D1553233

MR.
HEALER

Michel Tessier

To Mr. Healer Healing Angels!

Macha Einbender and Greta Fox

Illustration: Vincent Le Bee.

FROM THE SAME AUTHOR

In French:

- Itinéraire d'un Amendement voté
- L' Elevator
- Wagon
- Sagamore le dossier After Shave
- Mr. Healer
- Un Amour de Football

In English:

- *Wagon*
- *Disability Rights, 1985-2005 the Breakthrough Years*
- *Mr. Healer*

BIOGRAPHY

Michel Tessier is a photographer, author, and spiritual healer. When both of his parents died, Michel Tessier found himself with inexplicable abilities. He could tap into intuitive guidance and harness a deep, transformative power to heal trauma and fear.

Since then, Tessier has been exploring consciousness, connection and spirituality. He is a visionary for the highest good of humanity, bringing poised diplomacy, embodied wisdom, and expressive love to all in need. In these uncertain times, his voice is a much-needed guide.

Tessier is also a professor of photography with a passion for art, fashion, design and creative writing. He is the author of eight books available in French language, and three books currently available in English: *Wagon, Disability Rights 1980-2005, The Breakthrough Years,* and *Mr. Healer.*

For his contributions in the field of special education and disability rights, Michel Tessier was decorated as *Chevalier de la Légion d'Honneur* or Knight of The Legion of Honour by the French Republic President.

His first book, *Itinéraire d'un Amendement Voté*, was a finalist for *The Edgar Faure Prize*.

Michel Tessier lives in the United States of America.

"When I had nothing left to lose, I got everything.

When I stopped being what I was.

I found myself.

When I experienced total acceptance,

I was free to walk the paths of Energy."

Michel Tessier

DEDICATION

I am often asked about being a Healer and how I discovered my gifts. Honestly, I don't consider myself a Healer. I consider myself a man like any other man, living in service to humanity. I was chosen to share Light, Love, Healing, and the Worlds of Energy with others, so I do.

This book is my story. The characters, places, events, and incidents are real. Some names and identifying details have been changed to protect the privacy of individuals.

For my grandfather, David. I lovingly and graciously inherited my gifts from him.

For my mother, Anna. Although she has been gone for years, the dialogue between us never stops.

For my father, Maurice. Somewhere in this supernatural, my father looks down on us with infinite love he had for my mother and our family. When he left us at ninety-eight, he said, "Son, it's not age that matters, it's Energy."

This book is dedicated to them. *Death* has taken them, but in my heart, they are still alive.

Michel Tessier

1
MADAM AND MR. HEALER

"So, tell me, Sir. How did you start?" Anna asked.

Sitting in front of him, I place my cell phone down on the table, facing upward to capture the best audio. But before I had the chance to press record, he stopped me.

"Thank you, Madam, for not recording, filming, or photographing me, but please, take notes if you wish," he said gently.

I was embarrassed. He was right. I should have asked for permission to record our sessions well before this interview. I worried the infraction might set a bad tone, ruining the interview before it had even started, and quickly apologized. I could barely get the words out fast enough when he reassured me with a warm smile. He began talking.

"A long time ago, it was yesterday, or tomorrow," The Healer said with a wink. "We were in the car, I was taking a friend home. We had stopped in front of her house for a moment, looking at the stars. The sky was full of them that night. Suddenly, we saw a burst of light. Unsure if it was a satellite, shooting star, or UFO, my friend immediately said, 'I have a horrible headache!'"

The Healer took off his dark glasses and rubbed his eyes. I guessed it was a gesture to help him remember the evening better. My father used to do the same gesture.

"The headache was so painful. She just stood there, hands on her temples and tears in her eyes," he said. "I placed my left hand on her forehead, and touched the back of her neck with my right hand. Then my hands made circles in a clockwise direction, as the Earth goes around the Sun, the Moon around the Earth."

His words sounded somehow familiar as if I recognized them from a book.

"The Law of Universal Attraction like *The Secret* by Rhonda Byrne. Is that it?"

I asked.

I had tried to impress him with *The Secret*. It was a new best-seller, and I read it on the plane because it seemed like it would be good preparation for this meeting. I liked it so much I ordered the sequel, *The Power*, which hooked me just from the summary. *Perfect health, incredible relationships, a career you love, a life full of joy, with the financial means to become, do and have whatever you want, all emanate from Power,* it promised.

However, my words to Mr. Healer fell totally flat. They did not impress him, as I intended. Knowing I was not resonating, I became self-conscious. I felt confused on resuming the interview.

"So, what happened then?" I asked.

"What happened?" he asked intently. "With my hands, the pain disappeared."

I was quiet for a moment. "And since then, you've been healing people?" I asked. "Sir, how do you explain it?"

He laughed, raising his arms in the air. "It is my hands that heal!" he said. "And I am only the one who wears them. My hands emit a magnetic flux that merges with the atoms of my patients at the most intimate level, tracking and revitalizing the sleeping or sclerotic particle, even in very young people."

"And then?" I was eager for him to continue explaining.

"This fusion brings the body's tiny Energy connections and Aura connections back into balance, cleansing the Chakras, the real Energy centers of the physical body as they pass through the etheric body," he said.

I was confused, which I admitted to him. It all sounded very complicated.

"It can be complicated to explain what is natural," The Healer said.

"To say it more simply, what results is a cleansing of the organs, which allows the Energy to flow more freely. Is it clearer now?" he asked.

The Healer had an amused tone while sipping his coffee. The weather was lovely and people were walking by on the pathway. The soft breeze carried the scent of the nearby ocean.

He had arranged for us to meet for lunch at a café on the promenade. We were sitting on the terrace, sheltered from the sun, under large parasols. The restaurant staff knew him well and showed him respect. The Healer drank Americano coffee, and though focused on our conversation, had his eyes on the passersby.

He impressed me.

He felt it.

He seemed to enjoy my shyness, or on the contrary, put me at ease?

I was unsure.

It was not clearer though I nodded and said 'yes, much clearer' anyway. "The healing process is obvious to you, but for my readers, it is all new. It is a dive into the unknown," I said.

"You are right, Anna. I will be more precise," said. He put his sunglasses back on and resumed the conversation.

"In a few sessions, balance is rebuilt, and the Energy flows intimately. It quenches the thirst of body and mind, restoring the colors to the Aura, restoring the vibration of the Chakras and unraveling the disorders within molecules that cause anxiety, malaise, stress, illness and more," he said.

I was going to ask him a question, but he started answering before I had the chance, as if he already knew what I was going to ask.

"To be very clear - and this is very important - I never tell a patient to stop taking any medication prescribed by a doctor. I heal doctors and I refer my patients to a doctor when needed. That said, I will answer your question.

The Energy transmitted through me - also called magnetism - revitalizes the chakras and gives Energy back to the body of people suffering from various ailments, not to heal them, but to help them heal themselves. Self-healing is the goal for my patients," he said.

"Do you believe all Healers have this same goal?" I asked him.

"Well, each of us is different. I will not speak for the others," he said.

"Healers, magnetizers, bonesetters, dowsers, fire helmsman, radiesthesists, etc.

In my case, this *'Gift'* is familial. I inherited it from my grandfather, who received it from his father, and so on, since the dawn of time. I can go back without any doubt tracing it to the eighteenth century with a famous ancestor who lived at that time," he said.

"What was his name?" I asked.

"No, I'm sorry," he replied. "I prefer to keep it confidential. I don't want my ancestors to become a subject of research and polemics."

I pressed on, hoping he would submit to more details.

"I understand, Sir. But, how do you explain that you received this *'Gift'* when I did not, for example? It's a little frustrating since I'm equally passionate about the unknown world you describe," I said.

"Ah yes, I know, Madam. I read your articles and especially your latest novel, which touched me," he said. "And I would have loved to be given your gift for writing. That is why I accepted your request to tell my story, to share my art, he said. Not everyone can be a Healer, nor can everyone be a Writer."

"You say your work is art. Do you consider yourself an artist?" I asked.

"I say 'art' because I like this definition," he said. "Art is both a means and an end. You know the saying, 'the end justifies the means?' So, it is with the art of healers. There is no path to healing, healing is the path."

"Thank you, Sir," I said. "That was quite evocative. But you still didn't answer my question on why you have this gift and I don't," I said.

The Healer looked at me with a puzzling smile.

"Actually, I don't have an answer to your question," he said. "I've been searching for an answer for a long time, and I honestly don't know. I let my hands be guided by the mystery of life, the song of the world, the Great Spirit... Is it God? Is it nature where we are the leaves of the tree? The white cloud that gives life to the blue sky?"

He continued. "Do we have to explain everything? Intellectualize what lies outside the dictionary of academics? But, indeed, we try to name the unnamable! We put words on what is unspeakable! Concrete over abstract. Go and explain the concept of love, for example," he said.

The Healer called my bluff, and it must have shown on my face. I was terrible at masking my emotions. Sometimes if I pretended well enough, I could come across as naive, but mostly I had a bad poker face.

"You like stories, don't you?" he asked. "You grew up surrounded by books. Your father was a major magazine publisher. You followed in his footsteps, didn't you?" he asked.

"Yes, indeed, Sir. How do you know about my father? I've not said anything to you about him," I said.

The Healer did not answer me. He seemed to be fascinated by an older couple passing in front of us. He looked at them for a long time.

I asked him, "Do you see something special?"

"Can't you see? No, of course. You can't," he said.

"*Death* follows them! They walked slowly in rhythm, arm in arm, telling their life to Death who was watching them. The joys and sorrows, the travels, the births of their children, the death of their parents, their struggles to earn a living and support their families," he said.

"Death follows them!" he repeated. "It will respectfully wait until they have finished dancing their lives in this world to seize them."

I was impressed by how serious and respectful he was in telling me this scene.

"It's powerful and beautiful, Sir! It all sounds so real listening to you. But you don't answer me! How do you know about my father and my life?" I asked.

He simply laughed.

The evening was beginning to fall suddenly and the expression "happy hour," apart from special rates on food and alcohol, took on its own life. The evening presented an exquisite sunset, illuminating the background with a cotton candy sky. As the Great Celestial Artist boldly struck, silence fell on the terrace, leaving us all fascinated by so much beauty. Night had fallen.

The silence was soon broken by the sirens of the police and fire engines a few streets away. The red and blue flashing lights of the emergency vehicles illuminated the facades of the buildings.

The Healer united his two hands in the form of a prayer.

"The old couple!" he said. "They finished their dance. *Death* seized them!"

I look at him, stunned. By the time I grabbed my bag, I was a few steps behind him. I got up and ran toward the red and blue flashing lights, cursing myself for my choice of attire, the white dress I wore to impress The Healer and heels with soles as red as my lipstick.

"That's them," he said. "The old couple. They are lying on the ground. The rescuers are kneeling beside them and seeing there is nothing more they can do."

The Healer takes my arm as he puts his hat back on. We stand there watching the scene from a distance. The policemen made an honor guard for the couple.

"Look!" he says to me. "They are smiling! Their life must have been beautiful," he said. "*Death* brought them together for one last trip to the other world."

I look at The Healer. He is tall, fit, and has a nice look to him. The shadow of the Panama hat with the black ribbon on his head sculpts his face, enhancing the radiance of his gray eyes with gold glitter.

His white hair betrays an advanced age, and suddenly, the presence of my dead father is carried over to him. My arm comes naturally to take his, and so we silently return to the table where my dish and his coffee await us.

2
SANDRA'S AURA

"Do you know the writer Carlos Castaneda?" he asks me.

"As a matter of fact, I do. It just so happens that my father was passionate about pre-Columbian culture and stories related to the Aztecs. We had all his books at home," I replied. I was hoping to fool The Healer into thinking that I actually read those books.

"All right, then. You know him! You must have read his books," he says to me with a wink.

"Castaneda's mentor in witchcraft, Don Juan Matus, was a Yaqui Indian. The Aztecs claimed to be descendants of the Toltecs, called the 'Master Builders' at civilization's origin. On the other hand, only the Yaqui were direct descendants of the Toltecs."

I answer him in a strange high-pitched voice. "The Toltecs? I know *The Four Agreements*; I remember it by Don Miguel Ruiz:

May your word be impeccable.

Whatever happens, don't make it personal.

Don't make assumptions.

Always do your best.'

"Yes, Madam," he said. "In fact, Ruiz even found a fifth agreement," he tells me.

"Be skeptical, but learn to listen.'"

In one of Carlos Castaneda's books, it says, 'For me, there is only the pathway of the heart.' This is the realm where I travel. For me, the only challenge is to travel it all. This is how I work, always observing, losing my breath," he said. "Do you want an example for your article?"

"Yes, I would love one for my article!" I answered. "But you know, this could also be a book!" I said, hoping to flatter The Healer. "It would be a book all about you, of course."

I watched my father practice this kind of flattery when he worked in publishing.

"Yes, why not?" he said. "We'll talk about it again. And while you're waiting for the Pulitzer Prize, take notes."

His tone was firm, indisputable. I took a black spiral notebook and pen out of my bag. I must have looked like a university student with my glasses on, which I was just a few years before.

He smiled and took the time to finish his hot coffee, which the waitress had just refreshed. The waitress was incredibly solicitous, which made me curious.

"Sir, you are certainly pampered here. Especially by this young lady, no?" I asked.

"Ah, you mean Maria. She is an admirable woman and single mom who works day and night to raise her daughter. She had a health concern, which I was able to alleviate," he said.

"You want an example for your article, don't you?" he asked, bringing us back to the original conversation.

"Then, I'll tell you about Sandra, an art student who was brought to me by her aunt. This young woman, just twenty-three years old, was tall and attractive. She suffered from migraines, knee pain, and above all, debilitating patches of eczema. Sandra had lesions on her shoulders, arms, and legs, which made her self-conscious. She wore only modest clothing that covered as much of her body as possible," he said.

"She would love to have worn a swimsuit, t-shirts, shorts or pretty low-cut dresses. I knew this, but the unsightly legions covered her entire body," he said. I

"Of course, I knew. I felt sorry for her. My mother suffered from eczema and I knew how it made her feel," he said.

He continued. "You see, Madam, at Sandra's age, it was such a pity for her to feel so badly about herself, and in dressing so matronly, she denied herself of girlhood."

"How did you help her?" I asked.

"First, we spoke. I listened to her, to get familiar with her Energy. I could feel the Energy in my hands. I placed them closer to her body, just a few inches away, without touching her," he said.

"Sandra, your aura has atrophied," I told her.

"Talking to her, and with light hypnosis, I reworked her chakras. The crown, throat, heart, solar plexus, and root. In doing so, her Aura was reconstituted," he said.

I was curious about Sandra and what she might be feeling while The Healer was working on her.

"Could Sandra feel anything? Did she know what you were doing?" I asked.

> "Sir, right now I'm starting to feel you! It's like there is pressure inside!" Sandra said.

> "I was nearly three feet away from her, but she could feel the vibration pass through her," he said. "Sandra was better from the first session and returned to see me two days later."

> "Sandra, how do you feel?" I asked her.

"Thanks to you, much better!" she said. "My headache is gone, and my knee is no longer painful. My eczema attacks have lessened too, but those are still coming back."

"I know it's complicated for you. I was hoping you could tell me something, Sandra, for me to really help you. Did you ever have an abortion? It's important to know. It relates to your eczema."

"But how would you know that, Sir? I never told anyone!"

"If a fetus develops in the uterus, connected to its mother by the umbilical cord, its Aura develops within the mother's Aura. Terminations of pregnancies, however, can cause trauma. If a fetus is eliminated, especially through curettage, its Aura can attach itself to the closest Chakra, in this case, the solar plexus or navel. It causes the Chakra to stop flowing as freely. It can become blocked."

"Yes, it's true," she confided. "I had an abortion. I was so young, barely fifteen years old! I couldn't keep it," she told me in tears.

"You don't have to justify yourself, Madam. I am not here to judge you," I told her. I am here to help you put your Aura back in place and release the fetus's Aura. Your feeling of discomfort will ease, and your Chakra imbalances will feel restored. You will start to feel better," I told her.

After ten weeks of sessions, Sandra's eczema had disappeared entirely.

Sometime later, on a lovely spring day when the weather was fair, Sandra called me. She invited me to join her and her aunt for lunch.

"Let's celebrate," she said. Of course, I agreed. When I arrived, I saw Sandra sitting on the terrace of the restaurant. She looked lovely. I noticed she was wearing a little short-sleeved dress with no eczema in sight.

"Anna, you're crying," the Healer interrupted his story. "I'm sorry, I had a feeling this story might be personal for you. Is that it?" he asked.

I nodded, wiping my tears with my napkin.

"Don't worry, Anna. Everything is fine. The fetus was not meant to be, it was Karma. Everything is now as it should be," he said.

He smiled and put his hand on mine. All I could do was return the smile.

I was nervously looking for Kleenex in my bag when I saw that it had fallen under the table. I feel confused, clumsy. I bent down to pick up the tissue along with a lipstick that fell under my chair.

"Madam, you are not alone. I am here!" he says to me, sweetly. "Please, Anna, take your time and finish your dish. Order a dessert, no hurry!" The Healer raised his hat and motioned to the waitress.

I reacted as if I was waking up. Like time had stopped. I stood up and put myself together, mechanically smoothing out my dress.

I said, "Sir? Can we meet again tomorrow to continue? Same time, the same place?"

He nodded with a smile, and gave me a thumbs up.

3
CHANCE AND PERCEPTION

When I arrived, the Healer was waiting for me.

He was at the same restaurant we had visited the day before, sitting by a low wall underneath the shade of a palm tree. A baseball hat and sunglasses replaced yesterday's hat. He was wearing black jeans and a black t-shirt. His tanned skin and white hair reminded me of a rock star incognito.

Apart from my tennis shoes, I realize he and I were dressed exactly alike. He shook my hand and, with a gentle smile, beckoned me to sit next to him.

"We are dressed the same, Sir," I said. "Is it coincidence, or did you plan for that?"

"I'll let you guess!" The Healer said.

"What are the chances?" I asked.

"Nothing in this world happens by chance," he said. "Chance is when God walks incognito."

"I know that line," I said. "Paul Coelho?"

"Close!" he said, laughing. "Albert Einstein."

"Yesterday, we were different people, dressed differently. Today we are dressed the same. It represents our connection, how we are vibrating on the same wavelength, in the same space-time reality," he said.

"This resemblance can help us to mobilize the integrity of Energy. There is an inherent part of Energy in each of us, a part that neither grows nor decreases with the intervention of external forces. Diverse aggressions and the parameters of our culture and social environment mobilize every bit of this inherent Energy to obey established patterns of behavior," he continued.

"Energy is freedom. Energy is life. Either it is available to us in whole or in part, or it is unavailable, and it is Death.

We grasp this Energy in general and transform it into sensory data, and then we interpret this sensory data in the world of our daily life. This interpretation, in other words, is known as Perception.

We feel powerless to change our perceptions, which is why we feel stuck.

We repeat patterns. This is the reason so many people look to numb the pain, so often resorting to drugs or religious ceremonies or anything outside of themselves to find relief.

There is great pain in awakening. Change makes us uncomfortable. But to live, we must become comfortable with what is painful. We must embrace our discomfort, changing Perception.

4
MARY AND THE DEVIL

"Can we talk more about the concept of awakening? Do you have an example of someone who has gone through this process that you can share with me?" I asked.

"Come, follow me!" he said.

I do as he says, following the Healer. He takes us to a quiet street with a nice little park, a haven of greenery in the heart of the city.

"Let's sit there," he says and points to a bench in a friendly, shady spot.

It rained not long before we arrived, and the weather was pleasant now.

There was a sweet, pungent smell all around us, the scent that fills the air when raindrops come into contact with the earth.

We sat on the bench.

"Look at this person," the Healer said, as he pointed to a sleeping woman on another park bench not far away from us. She appeared to be homeless and asleep, her head resting on a bulky red and white checkered bag. She looked as if she was barely thirty years old.

"Have you seen her before?" I asked. "Do you know anything about her?"

"No, not personally, I don't. Energetically, I can tell you. This woman lives the life she wants. She reminds me of someone whose story I will share," he said.

"Mary, a twenty-three-year-old woman, comes to see me one evening. She told me that I had helped a mutual acquaintance. The first thing I see is Death lurking behind her back. I could see it in her shapeless clothes, her long wool overcoat, and her hair, which was long and dirty. She had a rotten smell to her, all indicative of her lifestyle," he said.

"Don't be surprised, Madam. I work with all kinds of individuals. It is not for me to judge them," he said.

"Oh Sir! Nothing you say at this point surprises me," I said, laughing.

"I need you to be serious, Anna. I just told you that Death was behind this woman's back! It is no laughing matter," he said.

Something in the tone of his voice paralyzed me for a moment. It reminded me of the KIAI of my childhood. I was just a little girl when my mother used to take me to Karate class. The teacher scared us silly with the story of KIAI, the spirit cry that kills.

"Excuse me Sir. How did you know that Death was behind her?" I asked.

"Death is always there," he said. It is as Carlos Castenada writes. Death is the only wise advisor that we have. Whenever you feel, as you always do, that everything is going wrong, turn to your Death and ask. Your Death will tell you if you are right or wrong, and that nothing really matters outside its touch."

"Death is everywhere," he said. "In the headlights of a car coming over the top of the hill just behind you. Visible for just a moment, then disappearing as if swept away in the night, reappearing a moment later at the top of a new hill, only to fade away again," he said.

"Death turns on the headlights, the same way we turn on the lights in our car. Then it comes for us at break speed, chasing after us. Sometimes Death turns off the headlights, but it never stops chasing."

The Healer looks at me for a long time, waiting for a reaction, but I have nothing to say. I'm terrified.

"This world is mysterious and frightening, Madam. Now listen to the rest of the story."

"Mary, tell me? Why do you come to see me?" I asked.

"I was told that you could cure me of this, Sir. Look!" Then Mary began to take off her clothes.

"Mary, there is no need to undress."

"Ah yes, there is. I want you to see," she said.

Once in her underwear, I understand. She has markings all over her body, bruises, and open wounds.

Then she showed me her arms. "Look at my veins," she said. "I smoke weed and Hash, and I do cocaine a lot, but I've never touched a needle. But now Jacky, my boyfriend, he's doing heroin because we need the money. And I've done things to the guys he introduces me to," she said.

"Mary, I understand. Now, get dressed, please!" I said.

"Sir, I don't have any money to pay you. But you can ask me to do anything you want. Whatever it is, I have no limits," she said.

"Mary, I am here as a friend. I don't care about the money, just get dressed. I will help you," I said kindly, and I meant it.

She looked at me with her big blue eyes trying to see my true Intentions. Then slowly, she put her clothes back on, as if with regret.

"I'm not used to this," Mary said. "In my world, you always end up paying one way or another…"

"Mary, in mine, your trust is enough. It pays me handsomely," I said. Come now, and tell me what you haven't told me yet. I can cure you, but I need to know."

Mary was in white T-shirt and khaki trousers. Her striped, rainbow-color socks had holes in them. She sat on the sofa, sitting cross-legged.

He watched as her eyes finally came alive. Then, she smiled softly. As the corners of her mouth gently turned upward, he couldn't help but notice how the gesture made her whole face light up. Finally, Mary looked like a girl of her age.

"Sir, my girlfriend told me I could trust you," Mary said. "You transformed her. I saw it with my own eyes," she said.

"I ran away from my parents, but they hadn't done anything to me. On the contrary, perhaps they were too oppressive. But it's not them; it's me. We lived in a nice house in the suburbs, in a good area," she said.

"In short, it was the classic story: I met a bunch of kids my age right out of high school who drank themselves into oblivion, smoking joints to the tip of their fingernails. They were living their lives going further and further to extremes. I don't know why, but I admired them and I liked it. I stopped talking to my family, old jerks who didn't understand anything."

"Go on," I said.

"I started abusing my family and stealing from them. It got to the point where they changed the locks and wouldn't open the door for me, even when I screamed and cried at the door! I haven't seen my family in three years. After that, I met a lot of other assholes, too many! And I did many stupid things, terrible things!" she said.

"Then, I met Jacky. He found me drunk and completely stoned in a fucking alleyway, lying on the ground behind a trash can like completely discarded, like a piece of shit. We found a place to squat, and with the money I gave Jacky, he bought some blotters with LSD. LSD is a potent chemical hallucinogen, Lysergic Acid Diethylamide, you know?"

"Yes, Mary, I know. And so are mescal, mushrooms and other…"

"Yes," she interrupted. "I know." She smiled, which was progress.

"The effect of the acid started very quickly. Everything was moving around me. My vision became red, and a giggling face appeared as if it was coming out of a pool of blood. It was coming for me. Long arms outstretched, hands with long fingernails like claws. It came closer and closer to my face; its eyes were blood red!" she said.

"Who was it? A demon?" I asked.

"No, worse than that! He told me he was the Devil himself," she cried out, terrified. "The Devil! That's him, damn it, that was him!" She screamed! "He was there to take me with him. To hell!"

"You have to help me stop the drugs!" Mary said. "I want to change and get out of this, get back to normal life! Please, help me," Mary said, and threw herself at my feet.

"Can you imagine, Anna?" he asked. I shook my head, no, and he continued.

I lifted Mary gently off the floor.

"Mary, Mary, of course," I said soothingly. I will guide you, but you're going to have to do the work."

"Yes! I am desperate. I will do whatever you tell me to do," she said.

It was the beginning of a long process together. Mary came to see me twice a week where we worked on her Chakra Energy. In just four sessions, she was getting better. But I knew that success would depend on her free will.

Alas, my intuition did not fail. Mary relapsed. Her friends offered her cocaine and weed. She broke down and felt very bad about it, but she realized she had to leave the squat and Jacky.

One day, Mary arrived, determined. She cut off her dreadlocks and gave herself bangs. Without the dreadlocks, she looked like a very young girl.

> "Sir!" she said. "I need a job and a place to live. I am ready to do anything!"

I found her a room with a friend who runs a boarding house for the elderly. My friend offered her room and board in exchange for her help there, and agreed to pay her a small salary.

From then on, away from the influence of her friends, things improved. Everything got better. Our sessions continued, one after another, until she felt free from addiction.

The next day, I was having lunch at the Grand Hotel Bar when Mary called.

> "Sir! I am in tears," she said. "I just can't stop crying!"

> "Mary, let it go! It's normal to cry, it's even good for you! You're human, you know! You've won your fight."

Drugs and his lifestyle had completely extinguished her feelings. On the phone, she cried uncontrollably, finally giving her emotions free rein. She was on the right track.

"Our sessions began in July. It took six months for her to feel released from the grip of drugs. By December, she had been invited to her parents' house for Christmas dinner. Our mutual friend took Mary to a department store to help her buy the right clothing. By the next session, Death was nowhere to be found lurking.

Then, the Healer stood up, clasping his hands together.

"I wish you a beautiful day," he said. And that was the end of the story.

"I wish you the same," I said. He got up to leave, but Mary's story was so intense I just needed to sit there a few moments longer. I heard the birds chirping loudly outside. I wondered if they, too, knew that Death was never far away.

5
THE FAMILY

The Healer lived in an affluent area, his house overlooking the bay. When I arrived, I found him sitting by the pool in a white shirt and pants. Coincidentally, we were dressed exactly alike.

"White suits you, Anna," he said.

"Thank you, Sir. Your home is beautiful," I responded.

"Indeed, it is gorgeous, but this house does not belong to me. Some friends host me when I come here to visit. Besides, what belongs to us?" he says with a big smile.

"But, Sir, our life belongs to us, doesn't it? Our body, our ideas, our thoughts…"

The Healer walked over to me. "You see, Anna, I've been watching the survivors. They taught me a lot…" he said.

The word Survivor gave me pause. I'm surviving breast cancer, the same kind of cancer my mom has, and unconsciously, my hand came to rest on my left breast. But I do not doubt he already knows about it.

"Life is the global whole that resists Death," he continues.

"Discovering is dangerous, but so is living. He who refuses to take risks condemns himself never to learn, never to grow, never to live. To be a slave of one's life is not living. The darkness of our past threatens the clarity of our present and future. Whatever happens with others should never be made personal; what others do and say is only a projection of their own reality," he said.

Changing the subject, I said, "Do you want to talk about family relationships? They matter quite a lot, I imagine."

The Healer answers me. "Yes, and they demand a great amount of Energy from us. For example, when you interact with your parents, you are the person they want you to be, not necessarily who you are. It is a game, and everyone plays it, even if unknowingly."

What was he talking about? "I don't understand," I told him.

He continued. "Look, a child grows up conditioned to play a certain role within his or her family. A child must act and do as a parent says. But where is the notion of 'self' in all of this? We grow up conditioned by our family to be who they expect us to be, but living like this requires an immense Energy expenditure," he said.

I raised my eyebrows. Was he talking about me specifically, or just making a generalization? I was becoming upset by the insinuation that I did not know myself; or was merely a pleaser. I felt very close to my mother, especially since my father died, and I was protective.

"How hypocritical," I said. "Children are always themselves, only they must abide by their parents' rules. I am not someone my parents conditioned me to be, I am me. There's no difference. I can assure you, Sir."

My response made him laugh softly. The Healer felt my sting.

"Anna, don't be angry with me, I am no different than you are," he said. "Believe me, I realized that I was a victim of conditioning, believing that my parents had the ultimate word and knew what was best for me. I felt the same way toward my teachers. It appeared that they knew what was in my best interest. Everyone else knew what I should be doing, or how to be doing it. In this way, I learned to trust others over my judgment. It was only in the search for myself that I realized what I wanted. I rebelled."

"Okay, but that's you, Sir. Not me," I said.

"Anna, let me finish," he said. "When I woke up and saw myself as a separate being from my family, the game unfolded. I would continue playing, only I stopped being the pawn my parents wanted me to be. I changed the rules of the game," he said.

"I no longer spent more Energy than was necessary on being someone else, continuing to pretend to be the same person I always was. Only there was no more pain. I even think I became a much better son than I was before," he said.

"Are you accusing me of being inauthentic?" I asked. "I'm not the one lying to my family or playing some game."

"No, it is not lying, Anna. It's about turning away from 'Love Sadism,' that's all. I had to develop immunity to other people's thoughts and feelings about me. The role I played only hurt me; and when I realized this self-awareness, I was no longer a victim of suffering."

There was a certain irony to his words.

Before coming to meet The Healer, I got into an argument with my mom, who did not want me to meet with The Healer alone. It made her feel uneasy. She pretended it was because a single woman shouldn't meet a man alone, especially not one I hardly knew, but

I knew it was something else. My mother didn't trust The Healer. Now I understood why.

So I lied to my mother about where I was going. It was easier than standing up for what I wanted, than telling her the truth. Instead, I pretended I was going somewhere else because I didn't want my mom judging me.

The Healer was right. I did play the game. And then, as if he read my thoughts, he said, "Anna, who is wrong and who is right, none of that matters. Vanity is nothing more than disguised self-pity. When we are too close to things, when we take criticism personally, we can't always see things for what they are. Perspective is all," he said.

"Let the other person take responsibility for his or her words or actions, which have nothing to do with you. Otherwise, you end up self-judging based on someone else's perception of you, not who you really are," he said. "The goal is to see things at face value, to have perspective. But a certain measure of emotional distance is required to do this."

"You want to do your best in keeping a distanced response, knowing your best changes from moment to moment. To do more than your best drains unnecessary Energy, but to do less, makes one feel guilty or frustrated. The trap is the race for perfection. 'I must' becomes 'I can' when we let go of the judgment and expectations of others," he said.

The cries from a flock of birds interrupted the Healer. He listens to them, he told me. They are recounting their deep joy of flying through the air, freed from the gravity of the visible world.

6
THE PAIN

"Come, Anna. Let's take a walk," he said. You are here not only to interview me for your article but also to be healed. Yes?"

"Sir, the two are not incompatible, are they? Are you able to take care of my back as we continue the interview?" I asked.

The Healer took my arm and guided me through the garden and toward the house. I was wearing white sneakers, a small black skirt, and a white T-shirt. As we walked, there wasn't a cloud in the sky. There was an air of deja vu. It was as if I was in another place and time; my vibration had shifted.

Suddenly, the sound of birds chirping morphed into the sound of cicadas in Provence, and The Healer was somehow my deceased father. What was happening? I was with my dad again. I could feel him and smell him, and suddenly my emotions became uncontrollable.

The Healer's hands moved to my back. I felt heat along my spine, only to realize The Healer was not even touching me. It was intense, though not at all painful. It was a strange mixture of love and pain.

7
TERESA

"It's incredible, Sir. My back doesn't hurt, after all these years...and the presence of my father! How did you do it?" I asked.

It was sometime later, and we had moved from the garden to the house. We sat in a large, comfortable living room with white walls, modern furniture, and colorful works of art.

As I sipped on a glass of iced tea, I noticed my back wasn't hurting like it usually did. The pain in my back, which I had considered a constant companion, was gone. It just disappeared.

The Healer looked at me with an amused smile.

"Sir, this is not funny."

"I apologize. I am not making fun of you. You just look so surprised. To answer the *Eternal Question* of, 'How do I heal? How do I do it?' The answer is that I do," he said. "I do, and that's it."

He continued. "At any rate, I'm glad you're doing well. We will need at least two more sessions for the treatment to be complete, for your back pain to be permanently gone."

"Of course, Sir. Not only am I no longer in pain, but I am totally relaxed, which I have not felt in such a long time," I said. "Tell me, are three sessions the usual amount someone needs to find healing?"

"There is no one answer for everyone. Some people need more, some less," he said. Some people stop before they heal. But rarely, it is less than three sessions."

The Healer sat across from me with a cup of coffee in his hand. He was dressed in faded blue jeans and a black T-shirt with elegant Italian blue leather moccasins. He drank in small sips; his hands well-manicured and powerful.

"Let me tell you a story," he said.

"When I lived downtown, on the first floor of the building, between the butcher shop and the bakery, there was a dry cleaner. There was a woman, Teresa, who worked there. One morning, she came to deliver my laundry, and when she handed me the shirts, she winced in pain.

"Teresa, you are in pain," I said. "You know who I am, don't you? Can I help you?"

She lowered her head, embarrassed, and answered me. "Yes, Sir, I know about you and the good you do, but I can't afford to pay you," she said.

"Teresa! It was me who offered to heal you. Please allow me to help you," I said. I was moved to see tears in her eyes. She blew her nose in a Kleenex and nodded.

At fifty-six years old, Teresa's back and shoulder caused her terrible pain. She could no longer work and tried remedying it herself with cortisone shots, but those only caused unwanted side effects and did little to alleviate the pain.

"I know I need to stop working for a while," Teresa said. "That's what they tell me at the hospital, but I can't do that. I need the money, my father needs me. I take care of him and don't want to see him in a nursing home. In my country, we take care of our parents."

I could feel her father's dignity in Teresa, and began healing her by moving my hands over her forehead. I focused on her third eye chakra while talking to her about our neighborhood and family.

"I have a 23-year-old daughter, Sir," Theresa told me. "When she was born, she was deprived of oxygen. She is disabled as a result. My husband, her father, couldn't handle it, so he left. I am a single mother caring for my daughter all by myself," she said.

"Sir, my shoulder is burning! What are you doing?" Teresa asked me.

"Nothing special, Teresa. Look! My hands are not touching you, I am at least two feet away from you," I said. "Remind me again, what's your daughter's name?"

"Clara, her name is Clara, like my grandmother. Now it's my forehead that's burning!" she said.

"Close your eyes, Teresa, that's good."

"Sir! I think I'm falling asleep. I am so tired…" she said.

"That's very good, Teresa. Your eyelids are heavy. Your limbs are relaxed. Let yourself go in the chair. When I count to three, I want you to sleep. Then I'll count again, and when I get to five, you'll wake up. You will no longer feel any more shoulder pain," I said.

Teresa's story so entranced me, it was as if I was there, too.

I looked at The Healer. "Did you hypnotize her?" I asked.

"No, not at all. We are in a bubble from the moment we are born. The bubble is open at first, then it starts to close, until we are sealed in it. The bubble is made up of all the ideas and perceptions of our family. We live inside this bubble for the rest of our lives. And everything we witness on its round walls is our reflection," he said.

"I understand what you are telling me, Sir. But, why did I see myself with my father and have such vivid memories of him?" I asked.

"This vision of your father on your arm, the two of you walking together. It jolted you," he said.

"Yes! It was so strange but so familiar at the same time! It was almost frightening now that I think about it," I replied.

"For the moment, you found stillness. You were able to calm your mind and block out the rest of the world. The sound of silence replaced your usual mind chatter, and my voice guided you to allow your inner guidance to start to take over. Then I cleared your Chakras, which allowed the Energy to flow more freely again," he said.

"I did the same thing for Teresa, which is why she can now iron without pain. After two healing sessions that we conveniently fit in when she delivered my laundry, she was cured," he said.

8
HEALED! MR. HEALER

"You seem shocked that I can do this?" he said. "Why are you making such a face when you know I am a Healer."

"Would you like some more tea?" he asked me. I remained very still, my mouth gaping open. With my cup in my hand, The Healer took the opportunity to fill it with more tea before I could respond to him. He laughed.

"I am glad to see I amuse you," I said sarcastically.

"No I'm not making fun of you. If only you could see your face! It is priceless."

He paused and added. "I can see that you're torn. You find it hard to believe this is all possible, is that it? That healing can be so simple?"

Annoyed at the suggestion, I shake my head to wake up myself out of this momentary daze. I put my teacup down, and as I stand up, my body moves quickly and fluidly. It takes a moment for me to realize the usual back pain in my lower back, that I usually feel when I go from sitting down to standing up, is not there."

An overwhelming sense of well-being replaced the irritation I had felt toward The Healer. I took a few steps forward, shocked that my body felt so free from any pain. I was almost embarrassed to be able to move with such ease.

I asked The Healer to point me toward the bathroom. The house was large and comfortable, decorated in a Mediterranean style. The high ceilings and open design made the home seem even more extensive. Bay windows, draped in curtains, let in a soft and soothing light. The floor was made of dark wood, which sharply contrasted the white walls filled with large canvases of colorful abstract paintings of portraits and cityscapes.

I was drained from all the emotions I felt. I couldn't wait to get back to my apartment to collect my thoughts and rest by myself.

Despite The Healer's invitation to stay longer and meet his friends, I left.

9
JOSY'S BACK

When I woke up the next morning, I was disoriented. What did I want to do today? Finish writing my book, work on this article, or drop everything maybe and just go to the beach? Good or bad, who's to say? as my mother used to say.

I get out of bed effortlessly. I am shocked at the ease with which my body moves. I can drop the soap in the shower and pick it up without the slightest pain, whereas yesterday bending forward that would be impossible.

The Healer had shaken the foundations of my daily life, upsetting my routine. I was a witness to surreal, supernatural occurrences and did not know what to make of it.

At breakfast, sitting on my terrace, I enjoy the ocean view while drinking my tea and nibbling on pancakes with maple syrup and fruit salad. I decided to take the day off and go shopping. The weather was beautiful, it was vacation time.

The streets were full of people walking by with their families. With sunglasses, shorts, and colorful shirts, the air was a mix of suntan lotion and the smell of the sea. It transported me back to my childhood and memories of eating Gelato with my father. The cafe terraces are filled with people enjoying the sun. I hear many different languages being spoken; the city transformed into a Tower of Babel.

What if life wasn't so complicated? I felt good, in perfect harmony with the universe. I felt younger, more beautiful, more sensual and free inside my body. There was a warm breeze against my bare legs, dressed in short white shorts and a matching white t-shirt. I felt alive for the first time since I could remember. I wanted to dance, to go out, to be in love!

I knew I had The Healer to thank for all this. I felt guilty not being with him today, not continuing to work on the article. But I needed to be alone. I wanted to enjoy my newfound sense of well-being and life without pain.

I decided it was a good idea to buy a new dress and maybe some accessories to go along with it, and thought of the perfect place. There's a little boutique on the corner of Main Street, right by the Italian restaurant and coffee shop I like. Next to it is a souvenir store that sells red and white lifeguard t-shirts, caps, key rings in the shape of multicolored surfboards, and license plates with all first names.

I stop by the coffee shop and order an iced Americano to go. As I enter the boutique, sucking on a dark green straw, I see that Josy, the saleswoman I know, is busy with a customer. She recognizes me and waves her hand. The customer turns around and waves at me also.

It is The Healer.

I was so surprised to see him! I let out a little scream, and Josy dropped a jacket in her hand, just as I accidentally dropped my iced coffee on the floor. Josy immediately squatted down to wipe up my mess with a paper towel. I moved to help her, but she could not get up.

"My back! Goddamn it! It's my sciatica," she said.

10
MIRROR, TELL ME...

I stand there frozen thinking, one moment you are standing upright and in perfect form. The next, you are sprawled out on the floor, completely helpless. Poor Josy is lying there, helpless to move. The Healer is next to her.

As Josy rolls on the floor, I see my reflection in a large mirror. I notice myself and realize I am so much prettier and younger than before. I look rejuvenated. I stand there, fixing my hair away and moving a few strands away from my face.

The Healer's presence consumes me. I wonder if he'll notice me - the man who knows everything, who has such power, who looks beautiful in a black suit complimenting his white hair and gray blue eyes.

Instantly, I feel jealous of the way he puts his hands on Josy's back and forehead. Jealous of the thoughtful way in which he speaks to her, touches her hands, and lovingly helps her get up off the floor. I am standing right next to him, and he doesn't notice me.

I can't believe it, but I am jealous of Josy and the attention he's giving her. `What a ridiculous and irrational moment I am having.

I feel like I am watching a movie in slow-motion. The Healer's hands move over Josy's body. He whispers in her ear, and I hear their gentle conversation about Josy's son and daughter, who are doing well and staying with their grandparents.

Josy intently focuses her eyes on The Healer and suddenly, her back relaxes like a bow released from its arrow. Then, she stands up slowly in disbelief.

"I can't believe it, but my pain is gone!" she said.

"Look, I'm standing upright, nothing! Nothing!" Josy said as she lovingly looks toward The Healer with immense gratitude.

"My God, this is incredible. There are no words to thank you. It usually takes me days to feel better when I pull my back out like this."

"You are most welcome, Josy. I am delighted that you are feeling better. Please come and see me for at least two more sessions, though. There are a few more things that I felt needed some work. But rest now."

He walked by me, gave me a huge smile, and headed to the door. "Anna, so nice to see you! Enjoy your day," he said.

I quickly ran after him.

"Mr. Healer! Sir, what just happened in there? Do you have time to explain it to me? How did you help Josy?" I asked.

"Time! Of course, I have time. It is you who wanted more time for yourself, no? I would feel badly keeping you from that."

But, how did he know? I never said anything about wanting time for myself. This man was such an enigma to me, and now in his presence, I didn't want him to leave.

"Sir, not at all! I was excited to do a little shopping for myself, that's all, but now after Josy and all, I don't feel so into shopping," I said. And it was true. I suddenly had no desire to shop. I only wanted to spend time with The Healer.

"If you are free, why not continue our discussions? Fortunately, I just happened to bring my notebook with me," I said with a smile.

He returned the smile and clasped his hands together.

"I would love to, but I can't," he said. "I have an event to attend. But next time, remind me to tell you Claire's story," he said and rushed off.

And there I was, in the middle of a sea of tourists heading toward the souvenir store. They were following their guide off the tour bus.

I feel sad, despite the blue skies and happy atmosphere around me.

Josy is on the doorstep of the store and calls me over. I tell myself that it would be a good idea to go talk to her, to get her story for my article about what just happened. Perhaps she knows Mr. Healer better than I realize? Maybe she can give me information about another aspect of him that I do not yet know.

But then I am overtaken by the crowd of tourists, now heading into Josy's store. She signals to me that she's sorry, she can't meet with me now, she has to go help the customers.

11
FINALLY, FREE

My decision is made. I will continue my book, and it will be a success.

It's unbelievable how important this man has become in my life, and in such a short time. I went from being a simple journalist to becoming hooked on healing and its power over me. I mean, it was miraculous what he did for me. To suddenly be free of the pain that consumed me for so long and without cortisone injections. It used to hurt just to bend down and put on my pants. That's gone now.

Painkillers, anti-inflammatories, antiseptics, antibodies, anti-aging - all these "anti's" became my friends, who allowed me to fake being normal, someone who just moved through the day like everyone else.

Thanks to him, I am finally free.

12
THE GAP BETWEEN
TWO WORLDS

I am lucky that my apartment has a terrace and a beautiful view of the ocean. Some days, the sunsets are so gorgeous they illuminate my soul. I had invited the Healer to dinner. He was fascinated by the sun's setting colors, which set off the color of his eyes.

"Remember, Anna! Twilight is the gap between two worlds," he said. These words gave me goosebumps all down my spine.

"It dominates in magnificence, and simultaneously, is a part of it," he said.

"When you say two worlds, do you mean day and night?" Anna asked.

"Yes, among other things. You see, Anna, we are surrounded by many different universes."

He had my attention.

"So, twilight would be a portal? And dawn, as well? To another universe?"

"I said a gap, not a portal."

"You play on words, Sir!"

"No, a gap exists by itself: we discover it, and we cross it. A portal is a door we control. We either open or close it, it's a matter of Intention," he said.

"Intention, what Intention?" I asked.

"Intention is life itself! It is Energy!" he said.

The darkness fell suddenly. Night came, and with it, an intimate softness that enveloped us like a comfortable blanket.

"Mr. Healer, I'm serious. What do you mean by Intention?"

"Seriously!" he replied. "Intention connects to Energy. It's like plugging an iPhone into the Energy of a circuit. When you connect to the Intention, it is Energy. When you connect to Energy, you can do anything. The vibration lifts you, the same way a chairlift takes you to the top of the mountain."

I laughed. I thought it was a joke. The image of The Healer on skis was hilarious to me. Here he was, in beige linen pants and a white linen shirt, I could hardly imagine him in ski gear.

I had told him that my dinner invitation was to thank him for all of his healing. He saved my life, which was a bit of an exaggeration but not far from the truth.

I wore a little black dress that night. I had champagne chilling in the cooler. I was well aware that my Intention was to seduce The Healer, but I was not as confident this was the same Intention he spoke about.

I started making jokes, trying to be smart to add to the conversation.

"Like a train on train tracks? Like a hairdryer?" I laughed at myself.

"But yes, you are right! That's exactly right! You and me, we are only Energy connected to Intention," he tells me.

"But what do you mean by Intention?" I continued. "For me, that's just deciding what I want to do, and then going to do it."

"Anna, you speak about Intention in the most ordinary sense of the word. There is a sacred, mystical quality to it. It is more symbolic than that," he said.

"Intention is a universal force that we feel, that we can see. It is Energy floating throughout the Universe, a force that moves through everything and is priceless. It's value lies in its abstraction. It is also intimately linked to man. In other words, human beings always have the choice whether to act on it, or not."

"We are far from the ski lift," I tell him.

The Healer laughed. "I liked the hairdryer," he said.

13
ENERGY, THE LIFEFORCE

It was getting cold on the terrace, so I suggested we go inside. I got up from my seat, motioning for The Healer to follow me.

"Come, champagne is chilling in the refrigerator, and there's salmon in the oven," I said. "I didn't know if you eat meat."

The Healer got up after me and took me by the elbow.

"I eat everything," he said. "It is not what goes into the mouth of men that is bad, it is what comes out of it," he said jokingly.

We moved inside for dinner, taking seats across from one another. I lit two candles and opened a bottle of fresh white Sancerre. The Healer was right, he ate everything I served him. He drank very little wine. I began to ask him questions, but The Healer refused conversation while eating. He explained he did not mean to be rude, instead he appreciated the sanctity of mealtime.

"The body graciously gets its Energy from food," he said. "Some religious groups say a prayer before eating or invoke grace. I don't do this, but I like what it represents because we are all in the same world, made of the same Energy."

"Let's talk afterward, he said. You can ask me anything. But for now, let's focus on this delicious meal you've prepared for us."

We ate quietly. Then, after dinner, we moved into the living room. I offered The Healer a coffee and cognac, which he refused.

"Sir, what do you mean when you say, 'What comes out of men's mouths is bad?'" I asked him.

"Everything is Energy, which is transmitted through vibration," he said.

"Let me give you an example," he said. "Imagine that vibration is like water.

Man can change the properties of water, right? He can make it hot or cold or transform it from a liquid to a solid or gas. Well, the same is true for Intention. Intentions also have power, they can transform Energy."

"It is up to the human being to act as a filter. He can transform Energy positively, as in 'good or white magic' or use it negatively, as in 'black magic.' The 'magic' is simply the Energy source; its power lies with Man," he said.

"This is why we must fear sorcerers or witches, who can easily be a jealous officemate, an ill-tempered neighbor, or the ex-wife of your lover. Those who harbor hatred or jealousy; or desire to possess something you have, can become a negative Energy source. This is what's known as the Evil Eye or Evil Tongue," The Healer said.

I am fascinated. Had anyone else said this to me, I would have dismissed it. But I had seen The Healer at work. I had seen his power, certainly in relieving my pain, and I believed. It was more than this; I had total confidence in this man.

"What happens to the people who get involved in negative Energy?"

"To demonize is to divide," he said. "It can create terrifying situations. Usually, a person develops blockages in their professional or personal life. Despite all their best efforts, nothing comes true. Nothing lasts," he said. "There is back pain, stomach pain, high tension, headaches, chronic fatigue. I'll let you imagine the rest."

"But fortunately, Intentions can also vibrate positively. This is called Power Energy, which can become a Prayer as well as a Blessing," he continued.

As he spoke, he moved closer to me, slowly placing his left hand on my back and his right hand on my forehead. He is so close that I can smell him. I recognize Eau Sauvage by Christian Dior, the same cologne my ex-fiancé used to wear.

I was so confused that I could barely concentrate on what he was saying. I felt like I had a fire in my back, but a fire that didn't burn - it was all Energy vibration. It was exactly like what he spoke about before with water - how it could be hot or cold at the same time. My forehead was frozen.

The Healer had the power to control the temperature of the Energy flowing through him.

14
FERTILE CATHY

"Anna, to show you what I mean, I am going to tell you the story of Elizabeth, a charming young woman of thirty-eight years old," he tells me, sitting comfortably on the couch cushions.

"I met Elizabeth one summer evening in an Italian restaurant in the heart of the city. We were seated at a round table. I was sitting between Elizabeth and another young woman, Cathy. Their husbands were also there. The conversation turned to the children. Elizabeth and Paul had two daughters and chatted away about them," he said.

"I noticed Cathy was silent," The Healer said. "Cathy's husband, Robert, told us that they had been trying for years to have a child. They consulted the best medical specialists in the country with no result. I could feel Cathy's distress," he said.

"But I could see Cathy was distressed over more than this, there was something else buried inside her. Of course, I knew what it was," he said.

"Discreetly, I whispered two words in her ear. This made Cathy begin to cry, at which point I handed her my handkerchief. Simultaneously, I took her left hand in my right hand and held my free hand over her abdomen. Paul, who knows me, tells everyone at the table that I am a healer who helped one of his employees with migraine problems."

"Robert looked at me skeptically. I could see he didn't believe in my healing abilities. He started talking about something in an effort to seem intelligent while dismissing me, but I didn't respond. I knew better than to respond at this moment. There was nothing to prove to this man."

"Cathy quickly apologizes to everyone, and excuses herself to the bathroom. Elizabeth follows her, and when they return, dinner resumes as usual. It was as if nothing had happened," he said. "As I left, Elizabeth discreetly handed me her business card."

"What did you say to Cathy, sir? What were the two words, out of curiosity?" Anna asked.

He had his annoying and mischievous smile. I didn't play into his game. I stayed very calm.

The Healer got up from the sofa and began looking at the paintings decorating my living room.

"And what about Elizabeth? Did she call you?" I asked.

"Yes, she called the next day. Elizabeth asked to see me right away and came that evening," he said.

"But I will leave you now. Thank you for this charming evening, the sunset was majestic and the dinner delicious," he said.

"You are leaving already? Just like that? You haven't finished the story of Cathy and Elizabeth!" I said.

"Yes, forgive me, I have an unexpected appointment. We'll see each other again soon, don't worry," he said. "I'm taking an early flight out of town tomorrow morning, but we will meet again soon. I will finish telling you the story then. Enjoy the end of your vacation," he said. "And take good care of yourself."

Abruptly, he walked out the door. I was so angry when I heard him laughing in the hallway that I slammed it behind him.

15
SALOMÉ

This is extraordinary, this feeling. I am discovering new positions that I was never able to do before. I could never bend like that without being in pain. I am experiencing an ease and sense of fluidity that is entirely new. It makes me so happy!

Previously, I had to wait until after a cortisone injection and sometimes prescription painkillers before my inflammation went down enough for me to take an Iyengar yoga class.

After class, I shower at the studio and walk out into the street. My hair is still wet, and I am wearing no makeup. I am in street clothes, holding my mat, as I walk by a canal. I am relaxed as I think about The Healer and wonder what he is up to. I missed him and wanted to continue my sessions.

And, of course, there he was. He was sitting on the terrace of a cafe right across the street from me. Was it a coincidence? No, The Healer would say there is no such thing as coincidence.

"Anna, what a pleasure to see you!" he said. "Come and sit down," he said with a big smile. "Did you enjoy your vacation! Wow, you look so relaxed, it must be yoga."

"I can't believe you just said that. You read minds now? Sir, how did you find me?" I said.

"Not at all," he replied. "I am as surprised as you are! I am waiting for someone. Oh, by the way, here she is!"

When I turn around, it is Salomé, my yoga teacher. She is all smiles and waving in this direction. I am beyond surprised to see her, as she greets both The Healer and me, and takes a seat.

"I had no idea you two knew each other," Salomé said. "Now I understand your renewed flexibility in yoga class," she said.

"Come and sit with us, Anna," The Healer chimed in.

"No, thank you," I said. "I don't want to intrude." Naturally, I was dying of curiosity, and though I hate to admit it, I was more than a little jealous.

Salomé is a beautiful woman in her forties. She has long, curly brown hair, big blue eyes, and a perfectly toned figure. In her class, she speaks calmly but with authority. She exudes a warm and soothing charisma, that along with her kindness, motivates us to go farther in yoga class. She gives excellent corrections and her smile is always encouraging.

Now that I think about it, Morris, the other yoga teacher, a friend of Salomé, first told me about The Healer. I guess that's the connection. I'll have to ask about that later.

"Congratulations, Anna!" Salomé said to me. "You did the whole class like a pro! I am really happy for you."

I'm trying to find out if she is sincere. Does she mean what she says? Is Salomé that perfect? I think to myself, yes, she probably is that perfect, which makes it hard to hate her.

"Sit down, Anna," The Healer said. "I ordered us green tea."

"Salomé wants to hear about Elizabeth, too," he said.

So, he was with Salomé last night? That must be it. I shiver. Was it a held sigh or a coolness coming from my wet hair?

"Well, thank you," I said. "I will join you for tea, and yes, I'd love to hear the story." Turning to Salomé, I said, "And I suppose he's already told you about Cathy?"

I can't help but imagine Salomé half-naked, wiggling her hips lasciviously, performing the *Dance of the Seven Veils* in front of the Healer, now King Herod.

I can't help but giggle to myself.

"Yes, she knows the story," he said.

He answered me in an amused tone as if he had read my mind.

"Cathy came to see me with her husband not long after our meeting to tell me she was pregnant!" he said.

Salomé chimed in. "Wow! And the healing you gave my mother the other night changed everything. Honestly, I cannot thank you enough for coming so quickly to help us. My mother was in such bad shape she could hardly walk," Salomé said.

"Salomé, I've known your mother for so long now, it was no trouble at all.

And I happened to enjoy getting back to the city," The Healer said.

"With you, everything seems so simple," Salomé said, putting her hand to rest on top of his.

"Ah, wouldn't it be nice if everything was that simple?" Salomé said, looking at me. I didn't have anything to say in response, so I just smiled and nodded, sipping my tea.

By this time of day on a Saturday, the neighborhood was bustling. It seemed that everyone was out for a walk on the street, in couples, and as families. The sky was so blue and the temperature so mild, it seemed as if nothing could go wrong. The cafe terrace quickly filled up, becoming noisy. A group of young students sat down at the table next to us, talking excitedly to each other.

The Healer stood up. I found him elegant, with his ecru Panama hat, open white shirt, beige pants, and navy-blue blazer. He came and stood in between Salomé and me, and with evident pleasure, took both of our arms in a motion to escort us somewhere.

"Come, my friends," he said. "Not far from here is a small park. We can talk more about Elizabeth's story among the people who are not people!"

In the same reflex, Salomé and I stopped dead in our tracks.

"What did you say?" Salomé and I asked at the same time.

"I said, there are people who are not people in that park. It was the case with some of our neighbors, too, but you wouldn't know it," he said.

Just as Salomé and I turned our heads, he stopped us.

"No, don't turn around!" he exclaimed. "You won't see them anyway. This world is much more complex than we think," The Healer said as we made our way to the park towards the park. It was situated just behind an old red brick building with the word "Boys School" written on it.

"Remember everything is Energy and vibration," The Healer continued. "There are force beings among us, beings who come from other dimensions."

"Some of these beings are benevolent. We consider them Guardian Angels while others are much more negative, more like Demons," he said.

"And others, they don't care about us at all. They have been living their lives since the creation of the Universe. Their vibrations can still affect us, though, without our realizing it. Their Energy they release is like pure water. It can be captured by the Intention of sorcerers, marabouts, gurus, mystics, and even those who pray," he said.

"Healers, too," he said with a wink.

"As I told you, Anna, Intentions are plugged into Energy like a ski lift pole on a cable. I know, you had a lot of fun with that metaphor," he said.

"Actually, I liked the iPhone," I blushed.

Salomé smiled.

16
ELIZABETH'S BEWITCHMENT

The park turned out to be a lovely square filled with flowers and a 19th-century fountain in the center. The sun's rays combined with the shade produced by century-old trees complemented one another. It created a beautifully balanced and harmonious environment.

The Healer took out his boxwood pendulum. He chose a nice wooden park bench, painted green, for us to sit on. He sat in between Salomé and me. We watched everyone enjoying a day in the park, mostly mothers with their young children.

"Sir, do we have people around us who are not people?" I asked him.

"Always, my friends, always," he said. "But some can become allies.

Mine guarantee us peace and serenity. They transform this simple place into a place of power."

"Is it relative to Elizabeth's story?" Salomé asked.

"Bravo, Salomé!" he said. "What a clever way to get us back to our story. Yes, it is, and it will help you understand how these vibrations are used."

"You already know the circumstances of my meeting with Elizabeth," he continued. "The day following our dinner, she came to see me. She was beautifully dressed in black slacks and a matching jacket. Her attire brought out the sadness in her pretty pale face and big black eyes."

"Sir, thank you for seeing me," Elizabeth said. "My friend Cathy was very impressed last night by you. She was the one who urged me to come and see you as soon as possible. She is worried about me."

"Elizabeth, please tell me in more detail. How do you feel?" he asked.

"I'm wasting away, Sir. That's the best way to describe it," Elizabeth said. "I'm wasting away! And I must tell you, I used to be an athlete. I could run marathons, swim in the open sea, pole vault... I ran the 100m at the Olympic Games if you can believe it! And now, well, look at me. I am only a shadow of my former self. I am a shadow of the woman I used to be," she said.

Elizabeth continued. "I have two children. I no longer have the strength to be active with my daughters, and, of course, the intense fatigue is also damaging my relationship with my husband.

You see, here I am talking to you, and I am already out of breath."

"Go on," he said.

"Bruises appear on my body without my ever having bumped into anything. And the most terrible thing, Sir, the worst part is this feeling inside my ears. It feels as though I'm on an airplane, or underwater," she said.

"In the beginning, it was only an occasional thing. But it happens all the time now and doesn't go away. It's terrible because I work with my husband in real estate, and I have to be on the phone all the time. When I can't hear anything, you can imagine what an ordeal it is," she cried.

Salomé and I listened intently.

"She saw the doctor?" I asked The Healer.

"Of course, she saw the best. She underwent testing and tried many things, none of which helped. No one could find anything wrong with Elizabeth," he said and paused. "As you can imagine, usually the people who see me have already tried everything."

I felt the presence of one of those negative forces we were talking about as he continued.

"So how do you help, when the doctors cannot?" Salomé asked.

"Well," he said and paused. "Dialogue comes first. Asking the right questions is a big part of it. In a way, it's like a police investigation where I interrogate completely," The Healer said passionately.

"Elizabeth, do you remember when the clogged feeling in your ears first started?" he asked.

"It was about 10 years ago," she said, placing her palms over her ears.

"Are you in pain?" he asked.

"Yes, and now I feel deaf but there's an irritating whistle at the same time," she said.

I was beginning to understand. "Did your fatigue, shortness of breath, and dizziness start at around the same time?" he asked.

"Sir, I never told you about the dizziness. How did you know that?" Elizabeth asked. "Yes, yes, you're right. And now that you mention it, yes, it all began around the same time."

"It was before you had your daughters, right?" The Healer asked.

"Yes, that is right," she answered. "How would you know that?"

"I know it now," he said. "Tell me what happened before you met your husband," The Healer said.

Elizabeth began sharing with him.

"I was very young when I met Roger. He owned the real estate company I worked for. He was handsome and charming, and one evening he invited me for dinner at his place. I was dazzled, naturally. I quickly fell in love with him. We were engaged not long after that," Elizabeth said.

"Business was going very well. We were selling a lot of homes, and one day I said how magical it was. He smiled at me and said I had no idea how true it was. He then said he wanted to introduce me to someone, so we got in the car and drove to a nearby popular neighborhood. There was a large and lively market there, very much like a souk," she said.

"The veiled women clearly found my dress and style inappropriate," Elizabeth said. "In the most unfriendly way, they began insulting me and giving me dirty looks as I walked by their stands. But then a tall man in traditional African clothing walked over to us, and suddenly, as if by magic, they stopped."

That's when Roger, my fiancé, introduced me to his friend, Le Marabout.

"Elizabeth, at last! I am delighted to make your acquaintance," Le Marabout said. "My friend Roger has told me a lot about you, but he was quite modest about your beauty. In turn, I would like to introduce you to Sara, my wife's sister," he said, ushering forward the young woman who stood quietly in his shadow.

"Sara's dream, you see, is to work in real estate," Le Marabout said. "I don't suppose you might be able to teach her a thing or two at your agency?"

"I was not sure why, but this woman, Sara, made me extremely uncomfortable," Elizabeth said. "Her smile and lovely figure were at odds with the cold, intense look she had in her eyes. At once, everything seemed wrong to me, but Roger, who was obviously overwhelmed by his friend, offered to bring her into the agency immediately."

"Please go on," The Healer said.

"I smiled at Sara, hesitantly, and was about to say something nice, but she was so obviously avoiding me and only looking at Roger. It was such an intense, insistent look that I almost felt embarrassed standing there.

On the way back to the car, Roger took me by the shoulders and said in no uncertain terms, 'Elizabeth, you must understand something. This man, my friend, Le Marabout, you have no idea how powerful he is. He is to be treated with the utmost respect. He is to be feared.'"

"Roger said he was a powerful sorcerer in his country, and now that he's asked for Sara to be a part of our business, our success depends on it.

I was sure Roger was exaggerating, but then he grabbed me by the shoulders, his grip much too tight, and looked at me sternly. He said that if Le Marabout asked him to do something, it would be done, no questions asked," she said.

"And then he said it was my responsibility to take on Sara, like my life depended on it. I must teach her, mentor her, and to show her everything she wanted or needed to know," she continued. "'You understand, don't you?' Roger said to me, in no uncertain terms."

"Elizabeth, go on," The Healer said.

"You must understand, Sir. I was shocked by what was coming out of his mouth. 'Roger, surely you saw the way this woman looked at you?' I told my fiance. Of course, he dismissed it, telling me I was crazy, that I was only imagining it. 'We do as he asks,' Roger told me. And that was the end of it," Elizabeth said.

"You understand, Sir, I had no choice but to go along with it. Not only was Roger my fiance, but he was also my boss."

Then, The Healer stood up and put his hat back on.

"Ladies, I must leave you now," The Healer said. "We will continue at another time. I apologize my leaving is in the middle of the story."

"See you soon and take care," he said, with his hands above his heart in a prayer position.

17
THE SIGNS

Salomé and I returned the greeting. "Namasté," we both said quietly. We then sat there, neither of us saying a word.

Just then, a blue and white ball hit my foot, and not long after, a little boy with curly hair came running over to retrieve it. His nurturing mother followed shortly thereafter with apologies.

The boy had a huge smile across his face. Salomé and I returned it, and then Salomé took a box of mints out of her pocket, offering me one, as they left us.

"Does The Healer do that with you too?" I asked, taking a mint.

"Do what?" Salomé answered.

"Leave, just like that! Without finishing the story!" I said.

"Oh yes," Salomé laughed. "All the time! What do you expect? He's our Healer, unpredictable but magical at the same time. One cannot exist without the other."

"Yes, I'll take him, and I guess you will, too," I said. "I mean, there are so few people who are people!" The complicit smile I exchange with Salomé turns into laughter.

Then one pigeon, then two, and then three come to peck at our feet. The wind blew the leaves off the trees, and that same ball rolled back to our feet. The little boy came to retrieve it again with a great burst of laughter.

We feel so content, Salomé and I, together and without words. We sit in silence like that for a while, and it is wonderful not to feel obliged to make conversation.

I watch Salomé follow with her eyes the little boy and his mother. I feel Salomé's sadness with a slight touch of envy. Salomé would have liked to be in that mother's place.

I raise my eyes to the sky. It was a sky of infinite purity, as transparent as sea glass. The first of the yellow leaves fell and swirled around us. The wind carried them high into the sky.

"The Healer would say, 'this is a sign,' I think," Salomé said to me. "I think it's time to leave."

Perhaps she was right. Unknown forces could be listening to us, like The Healer said. As Salomé and I stood up to gather our things, the rain began falling quickly. In no time at all, the sky turned ominous; the wind, threatening. This charming little square became a scary place.

Salomé said, "The vibration here has completely shifted, can you feel it? Look, I have goosebumps."

We used our yoga mats as makeshift umbrellas for protection against the rain, and ran off arm in arm toward the cafe terrace where we had finished tea not long ago. As the tropical storm raged on the city, we huddled together by the building awning, waiting for calm.

Just then, we noticed at the end of the street, an elegant couple walking together. The woman had one hand placed on the gentleman's outstretched arm, as they passed in front of us. She wore a dress printed in autumn tones, high-heeled boots, a hat with old-fashioned fishnet veil to shield her face, and an expensive-looking burgundy crocodile bag. The gentleman wore a three-piece gray suit, impeccably polished black shoes, a crisp white shirt and black tie, and a wide-brimmed black hat hiding his eyes. A pocket-watch chain hung from his vest.

"Get a load of this couple," Salomé said to me in a hushed tone. "It's raining buckets, and they're not the slightest bit wet."

"People who are not people!" I said. "That must be them. Look! They are here, but not here!"

It was the strangest thing, these people who were not people. It was as if they were quietly informing us of their presence. I was beginning to understand more and more what The Healer shared earlier.

"You are right!" Salomé said. "That must be it! We have to tell The Healer."

Salomé took my arm the same way the woman held her companion. "Look, it's nearly stopped raining," she said. "Let's go back to the café and have some hot chocolate. It's delicious there, very thick and sweet. You can tell it's homemade," she said. I was still in a daze as we went inside

18
LAURA AND LOLA

The terrace was practically empty, the rain storm having moved everyone out. The waitress seated us at the same table where we had just enjoyed tea.

"Laura, this is my friend Anna," Salomé said, introducing me to the waitress.

"Hello, Anna, it's nice to meet you," Laura said. "Actually, I think we've met once before when you were here. The Healer is not joining you?"

"No," Salomé replied. "He left."

"May I ask you how well you know him?" Laura said. She was a tall, thin woman in her forties. Dressed in all black, a piece of graying brunette hair fell softly into her hazel eyes.

"Anna is a journalist," Salomé said. "She is writing an article on The Healer."

"Then, Anna, if you are interested, I can tell you about how The Healer saved my daughter. It might be helpful for other teenage girls," Laura said.

"I would love that, yes, thank you," I said to her.

Laura looked out onto the terrace, now empty because of the rain.

"Come on, since there's no one around, I'll sit with you for a moment," Laura said.

"Well, and it's not because Lola is my daughter when I say it, but she is as pretty and smart as a button, which, speaking for myself, can be quite frustrating for the rest of us," she said.

"The Healer was sitting alone at the table you're sitting at now when I brought him the usual. Americano coffee, black. It must have been obvious from the expression on my face how tired I was. I had gotten a terrible night's sleep the night before, having spent the whole evening in the ER," Laura said.

"In my opinion, he felt your vibration," Salomé told her.

"Yes, you're right, that's what he told me afterward, too," Laura said.

"I realized I had forgotten to bring him a cold glass of water, so I went back to the kitchen. I returned, placing the drink on the table, and The Healer said to me so kindly that he could see how worried and exhausted I was. When I asked him how he could possibly know what I was feeling, that's when he told me he was a healer. He also said he knew it was someone else I was worried about.

"Yes, my daughter," I said. "Her name is Lola. She is 17. If you are really a healer, do you think you can help?"

"I would certainly like to try," he said.

"But not here. I get off in 10 minutes, will you wait for me?" I asked.

"Yes, I certainly can wait for you. At the end of the street, on the right, there is a square with a fountain. Do you know it?" he asked.

"Yes, I do, very well. I'll meet you there in 15 minutes," I said.

"Take your time, I will be there waiting for you," he said.

"Then he paid and got up."

Laura looked again out over the terrace to be sure it was empty from customers, and continued. She had our full attention.

"It was as if my prayers had been answered, like Heaven sent me an Angel!" Laura said. "By chance, my daughter happened to pick me up after school. She hadn't done that in a very long time, and strangely enough, doesn't object to going with me to the square. Then we saw The Healer sitting there, on an iron bench in front of the fountain. He got up and started walking toward us."

"Allow me to welcome you in this haven of peace, far from the hustle and bustle of the city," The Healer said to Lola and me.

Under his overcoat, he wore a black suit, tie and white shirt. I noticed a red ribbon on the lapel of his jacket, which my father wore. I knew it meant The Healer was a Knight of the Legion of Honor.

When he greeted us, his hands were together in prayer. Lola returned the gesture. "Namasté," she said.

"Namasté," he said.

"I'm sorry to be direct, but who are you, Sir?" Lola asked The Healer.

"I am a healer and your greatest enemy," he said with a bright smile. "We are going to fight, you and I!"

"Oh really. And, do you think you'll win?" Lola asked him.

"Without a doubt. That is, if you accept the challenge," he said.

"What's in it for me?" Lola asked.

"Your freedom. The end of your suffering," said The Healer.

"And what's in it for you?" she replied.

"Well, I get to see you and your mother happy. A family, again," he said.

Laura continued. "Believe me when I tell you that I've never seen my daughter like this before. She and The Healer answered each other like two dueling swordsmen. Lola looked at him as if he was The Messiah; he matched her in strength, and it gave her a sense of grounding."

"I have to leave you, I was invited to an official reception, but here is my address," he said and handed her a business card.

"Same time, this place, tomorrow - after school?" He left without waiting for her answer.

"Lola went to see him!" Laura said. "I couldn't believe it, but she did. For the first meeting, I went with her and dropped her off. The next time, she went by herself and was always on time."

"I asked Lola what they talked about, I was so curious," Laura said. "She told me they had philosophical conversations about life, or that they just discussed their day and how it was comforting to be with this man. She also said The Healer taught her about cleansing the Chakras, which I didn't understand until Lola explained it to me."

Laura turned to Salomé and I and said, "Both of you, being in yoga, must know about the Chakras."

We both nodded yes, smiling.

Laura continued.

"Lola told me about her Aura, and that he taught her to breathe. She laughed and cried with him... After several weeks of sessions, I saw my Lola change.

She stopped cutting the top of her thighs, she stopped hitting me during frustrated moments. She started eating again and most importantly, the suicidal thoughts ended. Within such a short time, Lola got her life back."

A tear fell from Laura's eye and I couldn't help but notice the lump in my throat, as well.

"The light returned to my child like an Angel touched her," Laura said. "She's so peaceful now, my Lola."

A few patrons made their way to the terrace, and Laura shook her head side to side, snapping out of the memory. "Oh, my goodness," she said.

"There are people here now, and I didn't even see them," she said. "Please excuse me while I take care of my customers," she said.

I got up and thanked Laura for sharing her story. I gave her a warm hug and felt so much compassion for this woman. Salomé followed my lead and took Laura's hands in her hands.

"And by the way, can I get you two ladies a drink? It's on me," Laura said to us.

"You know what I would love?" Salomé said. "Would you bring us some of your hot chocolate? It's delicious."

When Laura walked away, I said to Salomé, "Ha, an Angel. He would have liked hearing that."

"Yes, for sure," she laughed. "He would have loved it," she said.

Laura brought us the hot chocolate, so we stayed a bit longer, Salomé and I.

"How do you even know The Healer?" I asked.

"Pardon?" she said surprised.

"I mean, how did you happen to meet him in the first place? How did the two of you meet?" I asked.

"Oh, we met through friends," she said. "I was going through a very rough time. I really needed the help."

I must have raised my eyebrows or made a face at Salomé. Imagining her like this felt impossible. This woman, this beautiful yoga teacher who I wished I could be more like, seemed perfect.

"What? Don't look at me like that," she said. "This is very personal. It is hard for me to talk about."

I apologized and asked her to go on.

"The Healer was wonderful. Warm when I needed it, tough when I needed it. Mostly, he was there for me when I finally turned the page. He was my friend, and honestly, I wished I spent more time with him," Salomé said.

I smiled. "So you, too, were charmed?"

"Of course! I was alone and fragile," she said. "I had just broken up with a man and was feeling very lonely. Worse, I made it clear to The Healer that I wanted him, that I had feelings for him. It only proves his professionalism. How easy it would have been for The Healer to take advantage. But he didn't."

"You seem to be quite smitten yourself?" she said and smiled.

This woman is luminous, I thought. When she smiles, it comes from the heart.

"I don't know," I said. "I'll be honest with you. Yes, of course, I'm charmed, But, it's a very special feeling. I've been alone for a long time now, so, of course, I want to be in love. The Healer's warmth and charisma makes it easy to fall for him. He's obviously very attractive, despite our age difference."

I paused. "But I don't believe I am what he is looking for."

Salomé took my hand.

"No, it's not," she said. "He's not looking for an affair, nor is he looking to be paternal despite how protective he is. I think what he wants is to share with us the art of healing."

"He told me once he could not be a Healer if he didn't feel love. Love is what we all need, and we are mirrors of one another," Salomé said.

"I think you're right," I said. "When he came over to my house to do a healing on my mother's back, I remember him quoting Hermann Hesse.

'Every man's life is a path to himself, the trial of a path, the sketch of a path. No one has ever succeeded in being entirely himself; each, however, tends to become himself, one in darkness, the other in more light, each as he can.'"

"It was beautiful," I said.

Salomé stood up and came to my side of the bench. As she moved, supple and easily, she reminded me of a panther. She took my hand and didn't let go.

"Salomé, will you tell me someday why you needed him?" I asked her.

"You are so nosy, Anna," she replied laughing. "But that's your job, isn't it? To be a nosy journalist?"

"You know it" I said.

"Alright, then. Let me try," she said. "This is very hard for me."

"I met The Healer at an art gallery. Our mutual photographer friend, Alberto Rosso, had a showing there. At that time, I was an actress, or at least trying to be. I was working on breaking into the industry and my agent thought some nude photographs might look good in my book, as long as they were artistic. My agent introduced me to Alberto," she said.

"I agreed to pose for him. He had a reputation for being a very tasteful, artistic photographer, so I said yes," Salomé said. "Thankfully, the shoot went well. Alberto was a lovely man, he put me at ease. He was professional, yet demanding. To tell you the truth, I loved the way I looked and felt in his eyes."

I feel the emotion building up inside Salomé. She was on the verge of tears.

I took her hands while she continued.

"The photos he took came out beautifully. Of all the photos, one was very special. It was a black and white shot where I was in high heels and nothing else. My hair was up in a bun, held by my hands," she said. "My breasts, barely illuminated by a bright dark light."

Salomé continued slowly.

"The Healer had stopped in front of this picture," she said.

"He wore faded blue jeans, Italian shoes, a light blue shirt and a suede jacket. With his white hair cut short, he looked cool and elegant. When Alberto walked over to him, I followed."

> Alberto greeted him warmly. "Hello, my old friend," he said.

"Congratulations, it is a beautiful show," The Healer said, responding with a hearty handshake. He put his hand around Alberto's back in a loving way and reiterated, "Well done."

"This photo was taken with a Hasselblad, on film. The quality speaks for itself, doesn't it?" Alberto chatted. "I enlarged it from a print I made the old-fashioned way. I used Ilford paper, starting from a negative. 6X6."

"As Alberto and The Healer made friendly conversation, I was struck by how knowledgeable The Healer was about photography. I stood quietly by Alberto's side, waiting for a moment to introduce myself," Salomé said.

"The Healer glanced my way. We made eye contact and he held my gaze.

I wondered if he knew I was the woman in the photograph."

"Alberto, it is true, I do like your work," The Healer said.

"I can feel how passionate you are in these creations. You have the gift of capturing the beauty of your models' shape, as well as the grace of their soul. This photograph touches me very much."

"Precisely, Sir," Alberto said.

"Forgive me, please let me introduce you to the model. This is my friend, Salomé, the beauty who gave me the honor of posing for me," he said.

"Forgive me, while I leave you two to talk," he said. Across the room, he saw another patron calling his attention and left to greet him.

"What a pleasure to meet you, Madam," The Healer said. "I see that the photographer was able to pay tribute to your beauty and also capture a certain distress. Please forgive me, I am often direct, but it comes with the territory," he said.

"I am a Healer, as they say. But I'm sure Morris already told you that," he said.

Morris was a mutual friend, I hadn't made the connection until now. I had no idea what Morris told him about me and suddenly felt nervous.

"Ah, yes, what a coincidence! He has always insisted that I meet you."

"And look, now here we are. Life is full of coincidences," he said. "These moments that magically coincide. Put end to end, they form our existence," he said.

"Anna! It was crazy! I was in the middle of a near panic attack, and immediately The Healer knew I was distressed. Rationally, it made no sense," Salomé said.

"Go on," I urged Salomé. The story was getting good and I did not want to interrupt her flow.

"Excuse me, but how did you pick up from this photograph I was distressed? I hope it doesn't show outright in my expression," I asked him.

He remained quiet, holding my gaze a bit too long for mere strangers.

I was unnerved, but hoped it didn't show. My nervousness led me to talk a bit more, and definitely faster than I normally do.

"Sir, can you tell me. What is it exactly that you heal?" I asked.

"Do not worry, Salomé," he said. "I understand you feel a bit worried right now but there is no need. I am a friend. I am with you," he said.

"He then took my arm in a familiar way. Standing much closer to me now, his body exuded warmth and vibration. My fear subsided.

As I was no longer so nervous, I asked if he would like to look around the rest of the gallery with me," Salomé said.

"He obliged and then stopped at another photo, this one showing my bare leg, thigh and the sketch of my breasts."

"I really like this picture of you," he said, pointing it out to me.

"I admit, I was taken aback," Salomé said. The image he was referring to did not show my face, it was a neck-down portrait of only my figure. Unless you had intimate knowledge of my body, there was no way to recognize it was me in the photograph."

"But how on earth would you know that was me?" I asked. "There's no way to know that," I challenged him.

"Salomé, your vibration. I feel you," he said.

"Then we heard commotion from across the room and a voice shouting, 'GET DOWN!' Before I knew what was happening, The Healer threw himself on top of me, pinning me to the ground. I heard what sounded like firecrackers. I heard shouting voices but could not make them out," Salomé said.

"Panic was all around me. I was frozen. I laid there under the weight of the The Healer shielding me, unable to move if I wanted to. In what could have been minutes or hours, I had no idea which, until life started moving again in what seemed like very slow motion," she continued.

"At some point, the police came in because I heard sirens and ambulances, and the sound of the police telling everyone to lay down with their hands where they could see them. I was lying by the Healer. He had saved my life and made a bulwark of his body. I could smell his cologne, which contrasted the smell of fear coming from the bodies lying around us."

Salomé continued. "Who was dead? Who was alive? I wondered, as I looked across the room. I found Alberto's eyes, the photographer, he was not far from me. But his gaze was empty and a pool of blood spilled from his head."

"Oh, Anna, it was horrific," Salomé said.

"I cannot begin to imagine it," I replied.

"Anna, I had already lived through so much violence. I thought I was done with it. Then I heard a long, guttural moan. Who was making that sound, was it me? It was so painful it seemed to come from the depths of my being… and then very gently, the Healer lifted me up and carried me in his arms. He quieted me with his nearness, carrying me out of the gallery," Salomé said.

"He saved me. He saved my life," Salomé said.

"When we got outside, the scene was total chaos. It was like a battlefield. There were dead and injured bodies everywhere I looked. Police and rescuers were scrambling, talking to people on the sidewalks calling out for help. They were sorting out the wounded and who was left to be saved. The dead bodies were large black plastic covers," Salomé said.

"Cell phones were ringing everywhere, people trying to reach their families and loved ones. The Healer carried me slowly away from it all, away from this terrifying scene."

"Didn't the police stop you?" I asked.

"Surprisingly, no," she replied. "No one stopped us. It was as if we had become invisible. Were we invisible? Who knows?"

Salomé continued.

"The Healer gently let me down in front of a big black car. My brain was processing details out of order. My shaky body did not even react to being placed by the car. He opened the passenger side door and placed me in the seat. He attached my seat belt, and then walked around to the driver's side. He got behind the wheel and drove us away from the line of police cars and ambulances."

"When we got to my house, I suggested The Healer park and come inside, but he softly declined. He said he preferred to drop me off at the entrance to my building. 'Please come inside with me,' I begged him. I needed a drink and I didn't want to be alone. This man had just saved my life!"

"But then I went to kiss him, and he turned his head away from me quickly. Awkwardly, I missed his face, kissing the nape of his neck instead."

"Anna, I had my little black dress pulled up to my waist, my legs uncovered by ripped black stockings. I was as vulnerable as they come," Salomé said. "Never had a man refused to come up to my house, NEVER. Usually, I had a hard time getting rid of my suiters," she said and chuckled at the memory.

"So what happened then?" I asked.

"Well, very gently, very tenderly, he pushed away. I got out of the car, wobbly and ungrounded, as if I was drunk. Seeing me walk that unsteadily, he parked the car and got out, escorting me to my apartment. Then he helped me to bed, and left. He was a perfect gentleman. He didn't touch me," Salomé said.

> "I must leave you now, Salomé. I'm going back to the gallery to help, they need me there. I will see you tomorrow."

"Anna, you wanted to know how I met the Healer? When? Well, here it is! We met the night of the deadliest terrorist attack in our city."

I remained silent, so completely moved by Salomé's story. I could only take her in my arms and hold her tightly. As I did, memories came flooding back. That same evening, I was supposed to have dinner with a friend. She had to cancel last-minute, an act that invariably saved both our lives. The restaurant where we were supposed to meet was badly hit by the terror attacks.

Salomé snapped me out of it.

"Come, let's go to my place," she said. "It's just across the street. I'll invite The Healer to join us."

"That sounds perfect," I said. "Let's call him now."

"It is not necessary," Salomé replied. "He will know to come, don't worry."

No sooner were we comfortably resting on a terrace lounge chair, when The Healer rang the intercom. He ran upstairs to join us, like a young man. I noticed Salomé's black cat, who came to rub his legs against the chair, meowing and purring with pleasure.

Twilight was taking its time. A small fresh wind came to caress us.

In the sky stretch bands of colors from mauve to gold, the air was clear and easy to breathe. Suddenly, night arrived, as if projected by an invisible force.

We had bought sushi and strawberry tarts, to be accompanied by a glass of champagne. When we offered these to him, The Healer did not refuse. In the darkness, his eyes shone with what seemed to me like mischief.

"My friends, it is time to continue Elizabeth's story," he said. "I know that you have been looking forward to it."

He knew we were waiting for the story, it was as if he was gently taunting us with it.

"After my conversation with her, I became certain that years before, Elizabeth had been the victim of a spell put upon her by this professional marabout. It was like she was carrying some kind of object around, an object with an evil eye. Whatever it was, I knew it had to be close to her skin to work."

"I had no choice but to ask Elizabeth outright if she had such an object."

"Elizabeth tell me, are you wearing something that your ex-fiancé gave you? Maybe an item of clothing, or a scarf or bag? A piece of jewelry?"

She shook her head no.

"A ring? A bracelet or a watch? Remember, look hard!" I told her. I knew she had something, and my pendulum confirmed my suspicions, but Elizabeth had to find it herself."

"No, nothing," she said. "It was so long ago. I mean, he offered me lingerie, some dresses, but I left everything behind when I moved out," she said, looking at her hands.

"The engagement ring, I gave back to him… the bracelet, I threw that in his face," she said, laughing. "I broke a vase, but that was in the hallways…" Elizabeth said.

"You know, I found them together. In our bed. I was screaming, I was crying… and he didn't even look at me! He turned his head the other way," Elizabeth said.

"Go on."

"I ran out, slamming the door. He didn't even get up to follow me. In barely three months, she had certainly bewitched him. When this woman - this Sara - came to the agency, I showed her everything, I taught her everything!" Elizabeth said.

"And pretended to be nice to me! She pretended we were friends! But it was him she wanted all along!"

Reliving the scene, tears rolled down her cheeks. She wiped them away with her hands.

"Sir, I am crying so hard now I can't even see!" Elizabeth cried. "Please, I beg of you, please help me! I can't take it anymore"

I was sorry for all this suffering. I knew Elizabeth was in pain, but she had to be guided to find it herself. The evil spell was so powerful that she was blinded to it.

"Search, Elizabeth, search," I urged.

She placed her head in her hands to think, and as she did, touched her ears.

"Oh my goodness, the earrings. My diamonds! These studs!" she said, unscrewing one so I could see it more closely. "He gave me these earrings and they're screwed on, the posts are so tight, look. I forgot about them, I mean, I never take them off!"

"That's it," I said. "I am confirming it for you. Take them off, if you agree?" and he held out his hand.

Elizabeth was shaking like a leaf. She took off the earrings. The diamonds were pure, of a beautiful color, set on four claws and closed by a screw system.

"I remember! Sara was there when Roger gave them to me, they were in a red case. She asked to see them, and it was Sara herself who screwed the posts tight into my ears to make sure the earrings were on securely.

"Don't worry, I tightened them well. No chance of losing them now," she said.

"I was relieved Elizabeth found the source of her pain. Finally!" The Healer said. "But for the spell to be broken, the decision had to come from Elizabeth herself. It was the only way to put an end to the evil eye cast onto these diamonds by the marabout and Sara."

I told her, "Elizabeth, it is very clear. Do not hesitate removing the earrings. Unscrew them one by one," and she did. The right one was easy for her to take off, but not the left. The left earring wouldn't budge. It was on so tightly, I resorted to using pliers to unscrew it.

When I finally managed to remove it, she felt a terrible pressure in her ears. A pressure so strong that I felt it, too. She screamed and fell to her knees, her hands on her ears... And then, nothing more. Only silence..."

Elizabeth started to cry.

"Are you alright?" I asked her. "Can you hear me?"

"Yes, Sir, I can hear you just fine. My hearing is clear, it's not muffled or pained anymore. No more parasitic noises! I can't believe it," she said.

"This is a miracle," she said. "Thank you, thank you!"

"I knew how genuinely she meant it," The Healer said.

"Elizabeth came back several times. I worked on clearing her chakras, which all this aggression had badly blocked, and little by little, she came back to herself," The Healer said. "Her ears were like new."

114 | Mr. Healer

I expected a lot from the Healer, but this? It was huge. Salomé didn't say anything, she just continued sipping her champagne.

"But that curse on Elizabeth, it all happened so long ago," I said. "How did the curse hold so much power, and for so long?" I asked. I was so curious.

It was Salomé who answered me.

"Anna, spells are like viruses. If they are not eliminated, the host becomes infected. A person could die from it, these spells are so powerful. Even if the person who cast it died, or doesn't even think about it anymore, the spells hold power."

"Is this what happened to you, too, Salomé? Is this what you refuse to tell me about?" I asked her.

"Yes, but I told you plenty, already. Maybe one day," Salomé said.

I turned to The Healer.

"You must know, don't you? What she doesn't want to tell me?" I asked.

"I don't have to answer for her," he said. Salomé is free to tell you about her life, or not. It is not my story to share, I only tell with permission."

"So Elizabeth gave you express permission to share her story?" I asked, delighted to argue with him and perhaps catch him at fault.

"Yes, Anna. She did so that others would be less susceptible than she was, so that she might prevent other young women from falling into the dangerous hands of marabouts," he said in the tone of a school teacher.

"How crazy is that story?" Salomé said. "It's hard to believe it is true."

I was loving this moment. I never wanted it to end. I felt I had gained a sister in Salomé, and in The Healer, all of us together were... how can I put it? A new family. I was happy. It had been so long since I felt so comfortable, so included. I wanted to stay, but knew I had to get back to my mother. When I left, they remained finishing their champagne.

19
THE PENDULUM

The Healer lived in a quiet, residential suburb.

I parked my car in front of his house. To my surprise, out walked Josy, the salesperson from the boutique. Josy was so light in her step, she seemed to fly down the stairs, made even more impressive by her black high heels. She wore a short-sleeved white dress, and with her hair down, she looked like a young girl.

"Hello, Josy!" I said. "I am so surprised to see you! Look at you, you look absolutely beautiful and in such great shape. I am so happy to see you."

"Anna, hello! It's so nice to see you!" she replied. "I had some time off, so I decided to come and visit my family and some friends who live here, and of course, I wanted to see The Healer. This was my third and last session, which restored my chakras. I can't believe how great I feel," she said. "How are you?"

"Today is my second session," I tell her. "But I'm so much better already! By the way, we didn't get the chance to talk the last time I saw you in the store. It was so busy. But I'd love to catch up with you and get coffee sometime," I said.

"I would love that, Anna. Here's my number. I'll be here about a month, so we have lots of time to catch up, grab coffee, grab a bite to eat…" she said warmly.

We hug each other like lifelong friends who share a unique experience.

The weather forecast had predicted thunderstorms for the end of the day, but the sky remained blue and a small wind made her dress swirl.

Just to test out my back, I ran down the stairs when Josy left. I was wearing tight black jeans, ballerina flats, a white T-shirt and sunglasses. My body felt limber and light.

The door of The Healer's house was open. I entered and went toward the living room. I sit on a white sofa waiting for The Healer. Of course, he appeared in no time.

"Hello, Anna," he said. "You saw Josy on your way in? She looks great, doesn't she? Her healing is a great success," he said. "She'll be a wonderful mother."

"Wait," I said, as if I missed a step. "Is Josy pregnant? I thought you cured her sciatica!"

I amused him, and The Healer let out a great laugh, like he knew a secret.

"No, no, no babies," he said, laughing. "She's not pregnant, but she could be if she chose it. She can become a mother whenever she wants."

"I took the opportunity to settle her other chakras," The Healer said. "The mistake is that the body is divided and cared for in parts, with the mind treated separately. This is absurd because we are meant to be whole. We must heal and revitalize holistically."

He continued. "When Josy was very young, she experienced a major trauma. Sciatica was one of the consequences. Now that her chakras are realigned, her Energy can flow freely. Her suffering is over."

"Poor Josy, what was it?" Anna asked. "Can you tell me?"

"No, of course not, I am bound to secrecy," The Healer replied. "But, believe me, Anna, it was really horrible. I had sensed that there was something serious going on. I don't judge, it's not my place to do that. But I am human, so there are still times I find myself disgusted by man's Intentions. There are times I find myself in utter disbelief at the pain that people choose to cause one other," he said sadly.

"But, Anna, you know Josy. Talk to her. I am sure she will tell you, and then you can judge for yourself," he said.

"Of course. I will do that, we have lunch or dinner plans, I can't remember which but it's a reminder to me to confirm. I'll call Josy when I leave here," I said.

Inside, I could feel The Healer's anger rise at the person or persons who violated Josy. I could only imagine how difficult it was for him to be with his patients. His intimacy is his gift, yet I imagine it is a double-edged sword because he must naturally share in his clients' suffering. For a man with such empathy and hyper-sensitivity, there could be no other way.

"Are you ready, Anna, to continue your healing treatment today?" he asked me.

The Healer was as elegant as ever, and simultaneously casual in a sky-blue linen shirt tucked outside his faded jeans. He was barefoot, so I didn't hear him approaching.

"Yes, Sir, I am. You told me it takes three sessions to rebalance my chakras?" I said.

He was holding a small black velvet bag in his hand. He took out a natural wooden ball suspended by a black thread.

"It's a pendulum," he said with a smile.

"Yes, I've seen crystal clocks before, but a wooden ball like this one, never!" I said excitedly. "Is this a wooden clock specially made for you?" I asked.

"No, not at all! You can find it for sale on the internet!" he joked, and we both laughed.

"I just need to imbue it with my vibration. This one is boxwood; it is suitable for our session. I have other types of pendulum for different research."

"Please, have a seat, Anna."

I did and he moved closer to me. I could feel the warmth of his left hand, which he placed on the top of my head. In front of me, there is a mirrored wall affording me a glimpse inside the magic. The pendulum turned clockwise in his right hand.

His left hand moved down from my crown to my forehead. He stopped when he reached my third eye. The vibration was so intense; a mixture of heat and pressure penetrating deep into my heart. I could feel The Healer revitalizing my whole body, chakra by chakra, awakening them with renewed Energy. I could not help but think of the poem, "Leaves of Grass" by Walt Whitman.

> "I celebrate myself and what I say about myself is true for you, for every atom of me is yours as well."

Scanning my Aura, the Healer tested my Chakras. The pendulum moved in rhythmic circular motions.

At the height of my solar plexus, his hand triggered a heat wave through my back. The pain I used to feel, that old pain jolted alive again for a moment in a most powerful way.

"Ah, now I am at the limit of your Aura. It doubled in amplitude since the last time we met," he said.

His arms surrounded me about a meter away from my body. He did not physically touch me, yet I felt the intensity of his vibration all the same. And then I had the immediate sensation that I was falling. It was something like vertigo, only less disorienting.

"I feel dizzy, Sir," I told him. "Is this normal? Sir, what are you doing to me?" I asked and opened my eyes gently.

The Healer then placed his hand on my forehead and the dizziness disappeared. I closed my eyes again, calmness instantly restored.

"I have reactivated the Energy of your chakras, which are now all spiraling in the right direction," he told me. "Some were devitalized, but don't worry. We need one more session to finish that," he said.

I felt euphoric, as if I was high. This healing overwhelmed me beyond what words could describe. I took The Healer by the arm, using his strength for balance.

"I feel so peaceful. Please tell me another story, a nice story," I said softly.

He escorted me, smiling. He was happy to see me in this state of bliss. We walked out toward the garden, which was mostly pink and golden. A flight of colorful birds danced and sang in all their glory. The grass was so green, it was right out of a movie. Such loveliness sent a clear message, to the world and to me, of abundance, love and hope.

"What beauty, what harmony lies here," I said to The Healer.

"This harmony, as you say, is Nature's way. She gives us the model to follow, but leaves it up to us to follow it. As you can see, there is no useless expenditure of Energy. Everything is linked," he said.

"Our life is no different from that of a flower or a tree. As a writer, Anna, you must certainly know "Waiting" by Thomas Hardy?" he asked.

A star looks to me, and says:

"Here we are, you and I, each in our place…

What are you going to do about it?"

I say, "As far as I know, wait and let time pass, until my time comes."

"Me too," says the star, "me too."

"And me too," I said, if only to slightly provoke him. "I am waiting."

"Well, not me," he said, laughing. "I don't have time to wait, I have a busy life filled to the brim. Let's see, you want a nice story, yes? A simple one?"

"Yes, please," I said.

"Well, the truth is simple stories do not exist! Nothing is ever simple, is it? At the heart of every story is the suffering of a human being," he said.

The Healer took an envelope out of his pocket with two sheets of paper folded. "Here," he said. "For example, I received this letter just a few days ago. You can read it, that touched me quite a bit."

He handed me the letter.

Good morning Sir,

First of all, I would like to wish you all the best for your health, joy and prosperity. I come from Paula D., who is my best friend. She advised me to contact you, but the truth is, seeing the change in my friend is what pushed me to finally do it.

For a very long time, I have been under terrible pressure from my mother. But it feels evil somehow, the guilt she places upon me and the sense of obligation I feel toward her. I cannot help but wonder if it is a curse.

My mother's jealousy blocks me in every way. Professionally, I go on wonderful interviews only to never get the job. I suffer harassment at work; perversity and jealousy everywhere. In my love life, it is the same, I am blocked. I have someone in my life right now, who I love very much, but life continues to keep us apart from one another.

I thought distance might help things, but no. I left the city, my job and my friends to move miles and miles away from my mother. I moved to the South, and while technically I am distanced, emotionally I feel as pressured as ever. The tension only mounts and I have no respite, only continued telephone harassment, manipulation, pressure and guilt.

This leads to embarrassing physical and psychological discomfort, which I cannot control. I suffer from depression, fatigue and migraines, and I've gained a ton of weight.

Sir, I feel like I am completely lost in the middle of a storm. I am gasping for air, but there is none to breathe.

I can no longer see the path to take, nor the promised land. I honestly don't know what to do anymore.

Please help me. My only concern is logistics. Since I live in the South and travel quite a bit for work, I can only get back here on occasional weekends. Would it be possible for you to see me on Saturdays?

If yes, please let me know what I need to do to prepare. Please also let me know your fees.

Thank you kindly, and I look forward to hearing from you soon.

Sincerely,

Sofia G.

Like The Healer, I was also very moved. Sofia's story also illuminated the phrase I heard The Healer use a few times now: "The Other, the same as ourselves."

This woman, Sofia, could easily be one of my friends. Although some of what she said was quite specific, much of it was also universal. Any one of us could suffer from the same ills as Sofia, I thought.

Today, before practicing Yoga, I chose to meditate on "Leaves of Grass."

Here are the thoughts of all ages and all countries;

They are not only mine.

If they are not yours as much as mine, they are nothing or almost nothing.

If they are not the enigma and the solution to the enigma, they are nothing.

If they are not as close as they are far away, they are nothing.

"Tell me, Sir. This woman, Sofia. Are you going to see her soon?" I asked.

"Yes, of course! As soon as it is possible, as soon as she can…" he said.

20
STEPHEN'S SUCCESS

We left the garden and continued to walk until we came across a small recessed square with a fountain of water. A stone bench that looked centuries old invited us inside to rest for a while, and to share its immortality.

The Healer encouraged me to sit down. Looking out toward a fountain of cascading water, the birds sang loudly as The Healer said, "I want to tell my story of Healing."

I was surprised, but not too surprised. "Tell me, Sir, when people can't come to see you, can you treat them remotely?" I asked.

"At a distance? Yes of course! In another time and place, it was by letter-writing or photography. Then telephone. Now there's the live camera, image and sound," he said, showing me the latest version of his iphone. "It's magic!"

"In fact, just before you arrived, I was speaking with Stephen. And yes, he is a man. I have male clients too, you know," he said.

"Sir, please tell me! A man is very good for my article! Most people think that only women go to healers," I said.

"In reality, it is often true," he said. The women come to see me first. They send the men to me."

"One of my clients introduced me to Stephen," he said. "By age 34, he was an accomplished artist, having won major painting competitions, however, Stephen was a target for violent jealousy, or an evil eye."

"Since discovering it, Stephen found he had mounting health problems, as well as blocks in his emotional and professional life. At the request of our mutual friend, Stephen got in touch with me and made an appointment. But because his health was deteriorating quickly and he lived half-way across the world, we met by video conference."

"I will tell you about it," he said.

"Stephen was sitting on a couch in his living room. On my screen, his head and chest were framed. I put my left hand above him, moving it turn clockwise. In my right hand, I held my wooden pendulum, which quickly started turning in the same direction…"

> "Stephen, I want you to close your eyes and concentrate," I said. "Let me know as soon as you start feeling a vibration."

"Immediately, upon connecting with Stephen, I felt heat on my head and chest. My palms were burning hot. Stephen felt it, too.

"I feel heat," Stephen said. "I feel heat all over, and now I'm getting a strong vibration on my forehead. It's very intense…"

"The vibration came back to me, immediately signaling something was off. I had a feeling it was something ominous, which my pendulum confirmed."

"Stephen, do you believe in the evil eye?" I asked. He was not at all surprised, but rather, he placed his head in his hands."

"Yes, yes, I do," he said. "My mother always told me about it. She comes from a family in southern Italy, and always felt she had the eye on her."

The Healer paused and suggested we take a break. He needed a moment to refocus our Energy, he said, and left for a moment.

When he returned, The Healer said, "I remember one client, she had the worst time divorcing her husband. They were from the same region in Italy as Stephen's mother. There are very powerful people there, you know. One time I will tell you her story, too."

I said, "Of course! What's her name, so I remember to ask you later?"

"Claire," he said. "Remind me to tell you about Claire."

The Healer returned to the story about Stephen.

"Anna, the same way I needed a break now, I needed one with Stephen, so we stopped our session for a few moments. Upon resuming, some minutes later, Stephen was considerably more relaxed. He was drinking water, which had the effect of making me, too, feel more hydrated. I had been feeling extremely dehydrated before that," The Healer said.

"Immediately, Stephen's head starts burning up."

> "My forehead feels like it's on fire," Stephen said. "And the pressure on my chest is so strong, it's like someone is stepping on me," he said in a muffled voice.

"I maintained this pressure on Stephen for another 15 minutes or so, until the feeling diminished and I knew we needed another break. I was so close to extracting the bad spell, I needed just a few minutes more."

"After our next break, Stephen was very receptive to my healing. The spell began weakening and he could feel it. His chakras opened, and we both could feel the resurgence of positive Energy inside him."

"How do you feel, Stephen?" I asked.

"Like there is a warm and energetic liquid circulating throughout my body, starting from the crown of my head."

"There is a lot of pressure in your lungs still, though," I interjected.

"Oh, more than that, Sir! It's unbelievable pressure. There's a pounding on my chest, a knock-knock-knock, like someone is trying to open a door. There is a ray of light surrounding my chest, it keeps getting bigger and bigger, and stronger and stronger," he said.

"Don't worry, Stephen, it's your chakra opening and revitalizing, the Energy is coming to you!" I said to him.

"It's an intense feeling," he said. "You know those mint ointments, the vapor rub salve used for healings? When I was little, my mother used to rub those on my chest whenever I got a cold or the flu. My chest is feeling like that now, Sir. I haven't felt that feeling since I was a boy, it's like a part of me that disappeared is alive again," he said.

"Perfect. I'll leave you there, Stephen. We still have two more sessions to finalize this treatment," I told him. "See you soon." The pendulum stopped spinning. The session ended.

"So what happened?" I asked. "What was it?"

The Healer explained.

"Stephen's chakras cleared out. They all began working on their own again. The evil eye placed on Stephen, out of jealousy for his success, was gone. Later on, Stephen sent me a message saying he was so happy."

"The second session took place in two parts with one short break. At that point, Stephen had a deep cough in his chest with headaches in the mornings. I passed my hand over Stephen, and he responded almost immediately. He said he felt heat and pressure on his chest, which eliminated his coughing and turned it into a small scratch."

"But the pendulum warned me there would be remnant scarring in Stephen's chest, so I watched it closely. His headache eased as he felt pressure and heat applied to his third eye chakra. He described it like hot liquid lava spreading over his face, which was a good sign of healthy chakra activity."

"He was also still quite dehydrated. During the break, Stephen drank some water and it improved things, again. He started getting better and yet, all signs pointed back toward his chest. I could see the chakras inside him; we made an appointment for the third session."

The Healer stood up from the bench, and said to me.

"Come, Anna, let's go home. I'll tell you the rest as we walk."

The street was alive now with people after work and children after school, all eager to enjoy the good weather.

"I met up with Stephen at the end of that same week. He was tired since he works a lot. My left hand moved over Stephen's head while my right hand held the pendulum. Again, Stephen felt pressure in his chest. It was a burning sensation, he said, but not a painful one."

"The pressure extended to Stephen's neck, rising up along the line of his cough, and following the passages of his ear, nose and throat. It felt like it was the last bit of the evil eye. After a pause, I worked on his third eye chakra, between the eyes just above the bridge of the nose."

The Healer said, "Stephen told me he felt like a vacuum had sucked all the negativity out of him. When I checked the pendulum, it said all the Chakras had been restored, and the Aura was well-proportioned, extending around his entire body like a light-shield, protecting him."

"The treatment was finished; I was pleased, The Healer said.

"And was that the end? Did you ever hear from him again, Sir?" I was so curious to how the story ended.

"Yes, and in the meantime, Stephen received new professional proposals and the answers he had been waiting for.

21
THE GIFT

'To be able to heal over video chat or the phone, I mean, the fact that you don't have to physically be next to the person to intuit their thoughts or feelings, or to send your own healing to them, that is simply extraordinary," I said.

"I'm very pleased, it works. I've even found that sometimes the results are faster or more direct, to be honest. In any case, the result is the same in the end, and that is what matters," he said. "Often, when people are at home in their own familiar surroundings, they are more receptive, less inhibited by my presence or movements."

He paused. "With quantum physics, distance and time do not exist; there are no boundaries or limits. It is the same with my healing. It is the mystery of this Gift," he said.

"You explained where the Gift comes from," I said. "But not what it is, or what it feels like to have it."

"I don't own it, Anna. I received it," The Healer said. "And while I am proud and happy to be a recipient, it comes with great responsibility - great humility. A better way to see this Gift is simply that I am a messenger or conduit of it. I move Energy through beings on its behalf," he explained.

"For a long time, I have been aware of this connectivity. That's why mankind's pain is mine, the worries and joys - I share in them. It is the human condition as I, too, am human," he said sweetly.

The way he spoke was very touching, he was quite sincere. He saw himself as a Healer, transcended from a long lineage of Healers since the dawn of time, tasked with an important job to do. The Healer was not the man I thought he was.

When we first met, I thought The Healer had a great ego, like my grandfather. My grandfather was an impressive doctor, who walked the hospital corridors in a white jacket with a gaggle of eager interns a few steps behind him, taking notes. But The Healer was nothing like this. He was humble and considered himself in servitude. I had certainly misjudged him.

22
PEOPLE WHO ARE
NOT PEOPLE

We arrived at the entrance of the house, closed off by an imposing black wrought iron gate.

Everyone in the neighborhood was dressed in activewear, ready to walk, jog or bike. It was the kind of neighborhood where everyone barbequed together on hot summer nights, and actually greeted one another kindly as they walked to their cars and unlocked their doors.

"Sir, even in a place such as this. Are you going to tell me there are people here who are not people?" I asked.

"Yes, some are here," he said.

"Who are they?" I asked.

"Well, they are beings of another frequency. They live in several worlds at the same time," he said.

I remained quiet, waiting for him to go on.

"Some might call them Shamans or Witches. I will call them Sourcerers because they have Knowledge of Energy; they draw it from Source," he said.

"Please go on," I said. "Keep explaining this to me," I urged.

"In everyday life, we share a subjective state of being with other humans. This leads to being able to predict what people will do in given situations," he said. "Of course, we don't know exactly what people are going to do, but we can imagine based on a long but not infinite list of possibilities," he said.

"All we have to do is put ourselves in another person's shoes. Our shared subjective state is really 'Common Sense.' While views may vary from one group to another, or from one culture to another, it is sufficient to say the everyday world is mostly aligned," he said. "However, with Sorcerers, the shared state of 'Common Sense' does not apply. They have a different kind of subjective state,."

"You mean, essentially, they are like beings from another planet?" I said.

"Yes, in a way they are," he said, laughing.

"Is that why they are so secretive?" I asked.

"I wouldn't say 'secretive,'" The Healer said.

"Sorcerers do not see the everyday world in the same way human beings do. If we view their behavior as secretive, it is only because we do not understand it. We come from a different perspective as human beings, meaning we lack insight and understanding for how they perceive 'Common Sense.' So, we label it as 'secretive' and judge it," he said.

"But if Sorcerers are 'people who are not people' among us, they must do everything we do to fit in. Surely, they sleep, eat, read, go to work," I said. "So why is it I've never seen one?"

The Healer shook his head and smiled.

"You used logic and analytical thinking to conclude that," he replied. "They didn't hide anything from you, it's that you saw only what they wanted you to see. Anna, you could not see them because you vibrate on a different frequency, that is all."

I was starting to understand The Healer, but feigned being confused. I wanted to take advantage of his rare loquaciousness.

"Sir... are you one of these Sorcerers?" I asked. "Who are you in comparison to them?"

I hesitated asking for fear of offending him, but then could not help myself.

"Who am I? I am a Healer, and healing feeds on their Energy source. Remember, I am a conduit, which means I transfer their Energy to other beings to use for healing. I use the pathway of the Sorcerer's Energy to realign Chakras and restore human beings to their fullest potential. When fully restored, people can heal themselves."

"Is that what you did with me? You gave me the strength to heal myself?" I asked.

"Not strength," he said laughing. "Energy. May the force of Energy be with you, young Anna!" he shouted, laughing at his own bad joke.

23
THE ORIGINS OF HEALING

When I got home, I started a hot bath and decided to soak in it for a long while. Then, afterward, while cozy in my pajamas and white bathrobe, my hair still wet and wrapped in a towel, I allowed myself the pleasure of a chamomile tea and cigarette.

I looked down on the street from my window for "people who weren't people." I thought to myself how I had only just scratched the surface in beginning to understand Healing as an art. It inspired me to pursue my book and continue learning.

I smiled at myself, noting how this state of Zenness had brought me such newfound clarity and passion! "The willow paints the wind without the need of a brush," I recited to myself.

I got into bed and turned on my laptop. I searched for everything I could to learn about shamanism and healing. I knew enough to know that the practice was hardly new, it had been around forever.

Egyptian Healers wrote messages for patients, like prescriptions on scrolls of papyrus. These Healers were also known as physicians.

In Greece, Hippocrates, the father of modern medicine, used magnetism to heal. He called it, "the healing power of nature."

The Kings of France and England believed their healing power rested in their hands. "The King touches you; may God heal you," they said as they touched the heads of their subjects.

Paracelsus in the 16th century was the first to speak of the concept "Magnetism." A Swiss doctor, philosopher, and alchemist, he believed there was an inner life force in all of us, which lived in connection with different elements in the universe. He wrote, "Man has in him a magnetic force without which he cannot exist."

Two centuries later, an Austrian doctor, Franz Anton Mesmer, introduced Universal Magnetic Fluid. In this concept, a magnet is plugged into a source to charge. When fully charged, it then attracts and transfers Energy for curative purposes. Good health depends on the proper circulation of this Fluid inside the human body, so organs that are Fluid deficient become sick. Healing, therefore, restored the proper balance and circulation of Fluid.

Animal Magnetism or Mesmerism is related to hypnotism. Many modern healers continue to use it as a tool, allowing them to heal from a distance. Learning this reminds me of The Healer and Stephen, of course. I also remembered when The Healer told me about a patient suffering from eye problems, who he healed over the computer. During the Zoom healing, the patient said only her sore eye was crying. The other eye was completely dry. It was unbelievable to me, how The Healer could transmit Energy simply by waving his hands over a computer screen!

I fell asleep after transcribing the following in my notes.

"A Shaman was asked:

What is poison? Anything beyond what we need is poison. It can be power, laziness, food, ego, ambition, vanity, fear, anger or whatever.

What is fear? Non-acceptance of uncertainty. If we accept our fate, it becomes an adventure.

What is envy? Non-acceptance of the property in the other. If we accept the good, it becomes a source of inspiration.

What is anger? Non-acceptance of what is out of our control. If we accept, it becomes tolerance.

What is hate? Non-acceptance of people as they are. If we accept unconditionally, it becomes love."

24
ANNA AND MORRIS

I got up early for yoga, excited to see Salomé and take her class, but Morris was there in her place. I was a bit disappointed to learn Salomé was not teaching. It wasn't that I was unhappy to see Morris, I just missed my friend.

"Hi Anna," he said. "Nice to see you, again."

Tall and muscular, Morris' shaved head made him look like a tougher version of Bruce Willis. A former Special Forces soldier, Morris had his black belt in Karate, and was an expert in Krav Maga. His tough appearance contrasted with my vision of him as a Yoga Master.

Morris happened to be an amazing teacher. When he readjusted our postures, he showed tremendous knowledge, kindness and focus. As he put his hands on my hips, showing me how to properly square them off before bending to do Pyramid Pose, I felt a charge. He asked if I was okay, and I responded that it was hard to tell if it was actual pain, or just the memory of it.

After class, I sat for a few moments longer, letting my practice sink in. There was a tea room at the studio, so

I decided to relax and have a cup of tea there. The day ahead was an easy one, I could afford the time.

I ordered my tea and noticed Morris standing behind me in line. Discreetly, he told me I did well in yoga today, and he asked me about my back.

"I used to have such a bad back," I told him. "Yoga helps me so much."

"Were you in pain earlier, when I adjusted you?" he asked.

"To be honest, I'm not sure. I'm not sure if it was actual pain or just its memory."

"I completely understand that," he said. "You know, I have a perfect solution for you."

Morris took a napkin and wrote down a phone number on it. He said, "Take this and call him, let him know that I sent you. This man saved my life, there's no doubt he can save your back. I am serious, call him," he said.

"But who is he? What is his name?" I asked.

"The Healer," Morris replied, as he walked out the door.

This happened only last month, though it seemed since then that years had passed.

The next time Morris was teaching, I made sure I signed up for his class. There was something about him I liked, I couldn't quite put my finger on it. After class, I thanked him, and dragged my feet in getting ready to leave.

"You know, the yoga studio tea room is closed today, but there's a cafe across the street if you have time for a quick tea," he said.

This was the cafe where Laura was a waitress; I wondered if I would see her there. When we arrived, we naturally walked over to the same table I usually sit at with Salomé. While everything in the cafe was the same as always, nothing about me was the same since I was here last.

"Anna, your yoga has improved so much," Morris said. "I was very impressed today; I could see you working hard."

"Thank you," I said, trying not to blush.

"Hey, did you ever meet with The Healer?" he asked.

"Yes, in fact, I did! Your name made it happen, without it, I'm not sure The Healer would have seen me. It's not easy to get an appointment with him, you know."

"Oh wow, I'm glad," Morris said.

"The Healer worked on me a couple of times, and now my back is perfectly fine!" I said. "What an extraordinary man, he is. You know, I decided to write an article about him and maybe even a book."

Morris drank slowly. He listened to my words and looked in my eyes, but his thoughts were elsewhere. It was as if he was reliving distant events.

"How did you first meet The Healer, anyway?" I asked.

"It's a long story," he said. "It goes back years… When I was in the army, my regiment was deployed in Central Africa. My mission was to form a special forces platoon, selecting only the best commandos. One evening of especially difficult training, some of the guys decided to visit the hotel bar for a drink. We walked in and saw many expats there," Morris said.

"We ordered a few beers at the casino bar, which was right next to the slot machines. Later, at the restaurant, we ate dinner and had more wine. An orchestra on a brightly lit stage played Bob Marley."

I could imagine the scene and told him so. "Keep talking," I said.

"Next to us was a table with two European couples. The men had a lot to drink, they were laughing a lot and talking very loudly. The women seated with them seemed far too young for that scene. In fact, they were much too young to be with those men. I noticed the odd way they acted. The young women were silent with vacant-looking faces. I wondered if they were drugged," Morris said.

"One was a blonde with short hair. The other a brunette with long, curly hair. When the two of them stood up from the table, probably to use the ladies' room, one of the men grabbed the brunette by the arm. She screamed out in pain, as he yanked her hair and forcefully pulled her back into her seat.

"Where do you think you're going?" he said.

The young woman tried to free herself, unsuccessfully. She had tears streaming down her face by then. "To the bathroom!" she answered, sobbing.

She stood up from the table to try again, but he grabbed her blouse and turned her around. The young woman's blouse tore open and the woman was suddenly standing there in her bra. The man slapped her across the face.

"You belong to me," he said angrily. "Do you understand what that means? It means you ask me for everything, even to use the bathroom," he said.

"I watched as he violently threw the young woman on the ground. Instinctively, I stood up and my chair fell backward. I went over to the man and grabbed him by the arm."

"Hey, let go of me before I kill you!" he shouted.

"But as a trained fighter, I knew what I was doing. In just one blow, the man's left eyebrow burst open and his nose spread completely across his face. Two well-placed kicks, and I instantly broke the guys' kneecaps.

He collapsed to the ground moaning, while the young woman ran to stand behind me."

"The other guy seated at the table reached for the wine bottle, trying to break it over my head, but he missed. However, he landed a swift punch at the brunette, at which point my comrades stood up to take over. They grabbed the bottle and forced it down the man's throat, breaking his teeth. My comrades and I share the same values," Morris said. "You never hit a woman."

"Oh my god, this is crazy," I said.

"You have no idea, Anna." He continued.

"The men laid on the floor unconscious, and the two young women just stood there. The women had been trafficked, they had no idea what to do next. As the police came to the attention of the two bloodied men, we took the women back to the lobby."

"That same evening, we were able to arrange for the young women to be put on a military plane, where they could go home. Those two men were taken into custody and indicted with underage sexual and drug trafficking."

"While waiting for the plane to arrive, I learned the blonde's name was Lucy," Morris said, and then paused.

"The brunette was Salomé," he said.

"Salomé?? You mean, my Salomé? Our Salomé?" I exclaimed. "You must be joking."

"It is how I met her, our Salomé," he said. "And The Healer."

"She had PTSD, Salomé. Do you know about it?" Morris asked.

"No, I don't, and I'm not sure you should be telling me, either. This is Salomé we are talking about!"

"Yes, I know," he said. "We are very close, Salomé and I. You have nothing to worry about. Anything I share with you, it is only because I know she would not mind. I have nothing to hide from Salomé," he said, and continued.

"She suffered from terrible PTSD, which stands for Post Traumatic Stress Disorder. It is a disorder characterized by an inability to recover after experiencing or witnessing a terrifying event," he said.

"It can last for several months or years, with triggering events that bring back memories of the original trauma. Episodes are accompanied by intense emotional and physical reactions, such as nightmares and flashbacks, avoidance of situations that bring back the trauma, anxiety or depression," he said. "It happens all the time with soldiers in combat."

"My friend Abel, one of my closest brothers in the military, was a perfect example. He felt a sense of intense fear and helplessness when he got home from his tour. He had heart palpitations, excessive sweating and terrifying flashbacks. The simple sound of an exhaust pipe, a little too loud in the street, would immediately throw him down on the ground, ducking for cover. Later on, when he was back home with his wife and children, he was haunted. The need to be continuously on alert left him so anxious and depressed, he became suicidal."

I was overwhelmed by Morris' description. I knew exactly what he was talking about.

Years ago, I was assaulted in a parking lot. I trembled and cried for days afterward. When I told Morris about it, I still had tears in my eyes.

"I wonder if your back pain had anything to do with the trauma," Morris said.

"I wonder if your chakras were displaced somehow."

"Ah, our conversation, no doubt, put back in play by The Healer," I said with a wink. Morris laughed.

"Okay, let me finish," he said and I listened intently.

"One evening, William, an old comrade from our unit and the owner of a trendy restaurant we liked to go to, called me on the phone. He told me Abel was in bad shape, that he was drunk at the restaurant bar and acting dangerously."

"The bar was in the basement of the restaurant. When I arrived, Abel was in tears, collapsed on the counter, demanding another drink. William and I took Abel by the arms to help him get off his barstool without collapsing, and a man approached us. He was a man of a certain age with white hair and a short beard. He was wearing a nice blue suit," Morris said.

"Good evening gentlemen!" the man said, coming over to us.

"Above all, forgive me for disturbing you, but I was sitting at a nearby table and watching your friend. There is a painful feeling among veterans returning from combat, and I wonder if I can be of help to you," the man said. "I am a specialist in what is called PTSD, Post Traumatic Stress Disorder. If you allow me, I will gladly help your friend."

"Anna, I'm naturally very suspicious, and I was surprised to see this man appear before us like that, but instinctively I knew I could trust him," Morris said.

"Abel started protesting, but The Healer did not listen. He put his left hand on Abel's forehead, holding Abel's shoulder with his right hand."

"Abel," the man said. "I know you see the same scene, playing over and over again, like a movie. You drink to make yourself numb and to sleep, but it's no longer helping. There was nothing you could do to change things, you had to shoot those men, even at the risk of hurting other civilians. It was self-protection."

The Healer hypnotized Abel with his words and the vibration of his hands.

In a state, Abel said, "What do you know about it, old man?"

The Healer's hand had not left Abel's forehead.

"What I know is that you have been through hell, my friend. I can see it quite clearly. Trust me, it's all a matter of interpreting good and evil, and that's true for all of us!" The Healer said.

"There is a passage by Ludovicus de Santiago, The Healer said. It goes something like… *Don't make a distinction between right and wrong, because when you think you're doing right, you may do wrong, and when you think you're doing the absolute worst, you'll probably bring happiness to everyone around you.*'"

"Abel was calm now, his mind and body completely anesthetized. We carried him out to the car and thanked The Healer who gave us an address. He instructed us to bring Abel back tomorrow so he could help more," Morris said.

"And did you?" I asked.

"Of course," he said. "All of us were concerned and looking for solutions to our anxieties, our nightmares. This was the first sign that someone might actually be able to help. And then The Healer appeared, somewhat magically. Here was this man offering a glimmer of hope, a rainbow in our storms - he was an Angel among our demons," Morris said. "One by one, we went to see him. He relieved us of trauma and restored our energies. The Healer helped us get out of our constantly swirling and turbulent riptides, which all too often threatened to drag us to the bottom."

25
ABEL IN WAR

How did I, Anna, the little journalist, fall into this story? Why hadn't I continued to write romance novels or society articles or fluff pieces about skincare or makeup, for people who were people?

The Healer changed me.

In his presence, I had transformed and matured to the point where I sometimes had trouble recognizing myself. Was it possible he transformed what was superfluous about me into something more authentic? Was it possible all this rebalanced Energy inside me was so powerful it could turn my world upside down?

Who was this new Anna, sitting across from a charming and sexy ex-soldier?

I wondered.

Morris got up from the table to stretch. He then came around to my side of the table and sat next to me. In a bold move, quite unlike the old Anna, I put my hand on top of his hand. His skin was soft.

"Morris," I said gently. "What did The Healer do to help you?"

"Listen to me, Anna. Let's make it simple. It was pretty much the same for all of us, what he did. But as an example, I can tell you how Abel's first meeting with the Healer went. Does that work for you?" he asked.

"Ah, I see. If it saves you from having to talk about yourself, sure," I said.

He winked and smiled. He didn't have to answer me, I already knew he was more comfortable talking about Abel.

"What happened to Abel next?" I asked.

"Well," he said. "I arrived at the address The Healer gave me and right on time, like a good soldier. He was standing at the front door, waiting for us, which made me a little nervous," Morris said.

"Abel was first to break the silence."

> "Hello Sir. Thank you for last night, I understand you helped me quite a bit. But first, how did you know about my time as a soldier?"

> "Hello Abel. I know because it feels obvious to me. We are one and the same," The Healer said. "To know you, all I have to do is to know myself. I have been in similar circumstances."

With a wave of his hand, he ushered us to the sidewalk, which was shaded by tall trees.

"Come, Abel, let's walk," The Healer said. "It is a gorgeous day outside. Walking together is like brothers-in-arms, and this way we don't have to talk as much. I know you don't want to talk."

Abel felt comfortable with him. "I don't, you are right, Sir. Believe me, I've already talked to so many shrinks. I've been to so many since the army. It was often a woman I met with, and our sessions usually started the same way."

Abel took a deep breath and said, "I will tell you what I told them. During a patrol operation in Africa, I'm at the turret gun of the ATV. I felt the heat underneath my helmet, sweat running down my cheeks, the fear, the urge to pee. I kept my fingers wrapped tightly on my gun, careful not to press the trigger," he said.

"The road was dusty and it was hard to see. We came upon a village and suddenly, we were ambushed. The leading command car in front of us exploded.

We stopped next to the burning vehicle. My lieutenant grabbed his rifle and at the same time, commanded me to shoot.

"Abel, you shoot at anything that moves, you hear me? Cover us. We have to go and clear the commander!" he said.

"My gun just started shooting. I was spraying bullets everywhere. The driver remained at the controls, engine on. While our brigade went around to the back door, I fired shots to cover them. Somehow, the guys managed to get our comrades out of their vehicle and safely into ours," Abel said.

"We immediately turned around to leave. Passing through the village, the street was red with blood. I saw bodies lying everywhere. Armed fighters, yes, but also women and children. Civilians."

I looked at Morris and somehow in my mind, he became Abel. It was Morris I saw at the turret, the machine gun firing everywhere and at anything that moved. Bullets whistled around him.

Those bullets could have gone right through Morris, ripping him apart, tearing off a limb, smashing his beautiful face and covering his beautiful muscular body with blood. Then it would be Morris lying there on the ground, not moving. I couldn't help but become emotional.

Thank God, Morris was alive. I imagined myself taking him in my arms and holding him tightly, but I did not dare. He looked at me as if everything was clear, as if it were obvious. The Angel passed by and had brought us together.

Morris looked at me for a long time, as if he was discovering me.

"Continue, Morris, please. What happened between Abel and The Healer?" I asked.

"Anna, what a pretty name," he said, distracted.

"Alright, fine," he continued. "Abel continued to speak with The Healer."

> "I hated when they asked me, 'And what do you feel now, Abel?' What should I have said? That I felt an intense happiness at being alive, of having gotten out, of not being a corpse among these corpses? Or that I can still hear the commander, screaming in pain? It was such a mixed bag of emotions," Abel said.
>
> "And when I got back, I was so happy to be home again with my wife and children, making plans. But later, everything came back. I was haunted by the images of dead bodies, the sound of bullets firing out of my gun, the screams of

civilians and the smell of my gunpowder and sweat."

"It could just as easily have been me. One of those dead bodies on the ground, that could have been me. So now, I don't sleep because I found it's how I can avoid the nightmares. I drink to forget," he told The Healer.

"You see, Sir? I'm tired of always saying the same thing. Besides, it is always the same diagnosis, PTSD. And, for treatment, they prescribe psychotherapy, which does nothing for me. Talking and talking for what? Nothing. I tried antidepressants, but they just turned me into a vegetable."

"Of course, Abel," said The Healer. "Certainly, all the doctors meant well. They wanted to alleviate your suffering, we both know that, and their methods work for most people. You know, the western world is the biggest consumer of antidepressants. But they are the crutches of the soul."

A group of high school students sat down at the next table. I was afraid they would make too much noise and stop Morris from continuing his story. But, as soon as they sat down, they took out their cell phones and started texting. No one said a word.

Morris continued, undisturbed:

> "Abel had told me that he and The Healer walked around the block several times during their sessions. So that is what I expected, too, when I went to see The Healer," Morris said.

> "The peacefulness we enjoyed along the walk was broken by the sounds of a fire truck racing to an emergency. The Healer motioned me toward a shortcut to his house, which we took by cutting through a neighbor's large garden full of flowers and trees. The smell of freshly cut grass reminded me of summers as a boy, growing up at my parent's house."

> "When The Healer opened the gate, a German shepherd greeted us. I noticed two birds flying by, landing on a nearby branch. All the animals welcomed us, the elements all in their place. The world felt like it was in perfect harmony," Morris said.

"Anna, I spoke to The Healer like I had known him all my life. I told The Healer everything without him ever having to ask," Morris said. "Which was unlike me. And he listened, he really listened to me. He was with me, with us, on that day in the village. He knew everything, he saw and heard everything."

"We went inside and into his living room. There was a white sofa and large colored canvases on the wall. He brought me water to drink, and invited me to sit down."

"Then, The Healer puts his left hand above my forehead, his right hand holding a wooden ball that began turning at the end of a black thread."

"I looked at it curiously," Morris said.

"My pendulum," The Healer said with a smile.

Then almost immediately, I felt a pressure which morphed into a warm vibration. Several inches away from my face, The Healer waved his hand in circular motions, back and forth along my face and over the crown of my head.

I asked him what he was doing.

"I am checking the state of your chakras," he said. "My left-hand scans them and the pendulum shows me their state. If they are traumatized, they no longer turn, or they turn the wrong way. In either case, Energy no longer reaches your organs and the chakras cry out for revitalization. They know they must be revitalized in order to restore the path of Energy!"

"And how do you do it?"

The Healer smiled at me without answering. He continued running his hand along my body without touching me. He asked me to stand up and then he took a seat. He sat down on the chair, his hands turning in circles around me.

I feel Energy vibrating from my neck to my chest and long towards the solar plexus, to end up in my lower abdomen.

When he finished, I rested for about ten minutes on a couch drinking some water. After a short break, we started again until he was satisfied enough progress was made.

I made my way out the door to my car. I sat in the driveway for a moment, waiting for a garbage truck that was blocking me, and noticed myself whistling. I can't remember the last time I whistled…"

"It was this way for both Abel and me. Of course, nothing is perfect, long before the army, there was anxiety and stress, as is common for so many of us these days. But The Healer taught techniques for

166 | Mr. Healer

moving it out and boosting Energy to revitalize the chakras.

Whenever Abel or I felt this way, now we knew what to do."

26
SALOMÉ AND MORRIS

"This, Anna, is how I met the Healer," Morris said.

I looked at him as if he was a survivor, one of those everyday heroes who fights for his country, for his beliefs, to save others, just like the firemen or police, or that nurse I saw walking on the sidewalk outside wearing scrubs.

"What a story!" I said. I'm so glad you made it through, and that you're done with these wars. But, tell me, Morris. Where does Salomé come into it?

"When we returned from Africa, I knew I would stay in touch with these two young women. After exchanging letters, I learned that Lucy had gone to live in the mountains with her grandparents. It was too painful for her to be in touch, and I respected that," he said.

"When Salomé stopped answering my letters, I stopped by her address. The janitor told me Salomé moved about a year ago, but he didn't know where."

"My contract with the army was ending, and I decided not to renew it. I was done with war. My military life would now be part of my past, it was time to find work," Morris said.

"Some friends offered me jobs in security, working as a chauffeur, bodyguard, or security guard in casinos and big hotels. You know, the man with the earpiece? That was me," he laughed. "The work was simple and I was paid well, and most of the time pretty serene. I had a little jostle with customers from time to time, but it was nothing compared to the hell I had known."

"All my years of pay from the army, I kept in the bank. And I had inherited my parents' apartment, just two blocks away from the yoga studio. I used to stop in there for my morning coffee and croissants, and one day I found Salomé there. She was sitting at a table drinking green juice, dressed in yoga clothes with her mat rolled up beside her. She was alone reading a fashion magazine," Morris said.

"I thought about getting up and walking toward her, but I was reticent to remind her of her past. Maybe she didn't want to be in touch, after all, she never tried to find me when she moved. It was complicated," he said.

Then Salomé found me. Her eyes locked into mine, like destiny.

"Morris! Is that you?" she said. "What a surprise!"

"I made my way toward her and she threw herself into my arms for a warm embrace."

"Salomé! I can't believe it's you! I looked all over for you when I didn't hear from you. I sent letters, I even went to your house, but they told me you moved without leaving an address."

"Ah! I'm so sorry, I didn't know! You know, it was so hard... I went to my parents' house in the country. I didn't want to think anymore about what I had been through; I just wanted a new life."

"Do you come to this café often?" Morris asked. "Because I happen to live right next door, so I have breakfast here almost every morning."

"Morris, it's so nice to see you. You know, I've thought about you often and I'm so happy to see you here."

I could tell, she was genuinely happy to see me. She asked about all my comrades and whether I had spoken to Lucy. Salomé thought that Lucy may have gone much farther than her grandparents house, maybe even returning to Africa.

"You must not blame Lucy," Salomé said. "There are forces out there that catch us and force us to do what they want. Lucy is weak! Much more fragile than I am, I am a fighter. If only I didn't have the terrible nightmares that remind me of who I once was."

"I have the same recurring nightmare, it's silly."

"Tell me, Salomé. I have nightmares, too."

"Well, in this one dream, a witch comes for me and tells me we are going to the forest. 'Come, I have been waiting for you! We are all waiting for you,' she said with an evil laugh. That laugh frightens me terribly, and I wake up trembling and soaked in my own sweat," Salomé said.

"Yoga helps a lot," she said.

"Anna, anyone who spends time in Africa knows the potential of sorcerers. I had no idea of their power and influence until I traveled there, so, of course, I believed every word Salomé told me," Morris said. "Have you been to Africa before?"

"Yes, one time. I traveled to Côte d'Ivoire, spending ten days at a Club Med there. When I was there, I visited the nearby villages in Abidjan, which fascinated me. I could tell the atmosphere, or the 'vibration' as The Healer would say, was most definitely charged."

"I told Salomé about Abel and my experience with The Healer, and suggested she try a few sessions; however, she was not interested and I had no desire to convince her of anything. She was finished with 'powerful men' and wizardry of all kinds, she told me. I understood. After all she had been through, she said she was actually finished with men altogether."

I underwood that. Poor Salomé.

"Anna, what she went through... no one should suffer it. All I wanted was to be near her, to protect her and keep her safe. I just wanted to stay with her, sit next to her, and if she allowed it, take her hand and smile at her. Anything to make her feel I was with her," Morris said.

I was looking at him with new eyes. Morris seemed so at peace with himself, so grounded. He radiated a vibration so positive that I felt it, too. He was beautiful, his soul was beautiful! I was moved.

And yet, to think that last time I saw him, when I was so disappointed, he was substituting for Salomé. I was so wrong about this man. He was so strong and reassuring, and how easy it would be to fall in love with him, I thought. Since his story, I felt I knew his soul. Beneath that muscled exterior was a gentleness and warmth that is hard to find.

I thought about The Healer... Few people paid as much attention to me as he did. My father had died when I was young, and my mother remarried several times to dominant men. The last one put me in boarding school, far away from home, where I spent years feeling lonely.

But The Healer was more like a father figure now. I loved him, but this was different. I was grateful for this man and hoped to have a forever-friendship. I realized in meeting The Healer, how long I had looked for someone to love and protect me...

And here I was looking at Morris in a way that was nothing like my feelings for The Healer. My God, if he only knew what I was thinking.

Morris continued.

"I decided to sign up for Salomé's yoga classes. Then, when she saw my ability, she had me sub for her a few times, mostly when her back was hurting her. Like you, Anna, she had back pain."

"Then, I started teaching Karate and Aikido classes at the studio. I found I really enjoyed teaching, and anything to spend more time with Salomé felt good. We saw each other a lot. She started to trust me."

"Time passed, I didn't dare tell Salomé I was developing feelings for her. I was afraid that she wouldn't want to see me anymore," Morris said. "But one night she invited me over for dinner, and I stayed the night."

"Salomé used to wake up terrified in the middle of the night, and always around 3:00 am. It broke my heart to see her suffer like that. I begged her to see The Healer, but she continued to refuse."

"Finally, I spoke to The Healer about her," Morris said.

"Don't worry about Salomé, Morris. I am here for her whenever she is ready. Everything will be okay," The Healer told me.

"And, as you know Anna, he went to meet her at the photographer's opening the night of that terrible attack. I felt so bad I hadn't joined her that night, but I was working that night, helping Abel on a security assignment."

"Morris, for all you know, you could have been killed that night!" I said. I trembled, imagining him and Salomé in a pool of blood.

"Luckily," Morris said, "The Healer was there. He was with her, protecting her and taking care of her. I never found out how he managed to free her and leave the scene, but it didn't matter. All I know is that in a few short weeks, Salomé's nightmares and back pain were gone. It was a miracle."

I had a pit in my stomach thinking about Salomé and Morris together. It was a blow, seeing this man who I was developing such strong feelings for, having feelings for my friend.

I apologized and took a moment to freshen up in the bathroom. I need to pull myself together.

When I returned, I asked innocently. "Did you marry her?"

"Oh no, not at all, it was nothing like that," Morris said.

"It didn't last very long. It was a brief affair, very intense but short lived. It was almost as if Salomé needed me for an Energy release to get back on track. After she met The Healer, she was quick to move on from me. I understood it, I understood her," Morris said.

"We stayed close, but as friends," he said. "And when she said she was finished with men, she meant it," he laughed. "Did you know Salomé is thinking of marrying another woman? They are very happy together, actually, they met in yoga."

They are no longer together? I felt a weight come off my shoulders.

"I'm sorry that you and Salomé didn't work out, Morris," I said. "Does that mean you are single? Or is there someone else in your life?"

"I am single," he said, both amused and a little perplexed. "Any more questions, Sherlock"?"

I smiled, hoping there was a chance for us. I felt a ball of heat, radiating throughout my body. It was a pleasant sensation, and it must have been noticeable because I could feel myself blushing.

I finished my glass of water filled with ice cubes.

What do you know? A woman, Salomé was going to marry a woman. It was beautiful thinking of Salomé happy.

I wondered if she would mind me dating Morris. You never know with these things.

On the taxi ride home from the cafe, I found myself whistling, like Abel.

27
ENEMIES

Witchcraft is often involved with matters of healing, fate, and other spiritual activities. But in reality, its main occupation is war. You see it everywhere, in Miami, New York and Los Angeles, wherever there are brujos, hugans, curandos and santeros among practicing immigrant communities. Most homicides, in fact, were directly or indirectly related to witchcraft.

There were, of course, saints and wise men among the shamans. But there were few of them among generals, politicians and corporations.

I had trouble falling asleep after reading Michael Gruber's novel, "Tropic of Night." I had been devouring magic books from all over the world, and felt constantly surrounded by wizards - those people who aren't people. I wondered what The Healer would think of it.

The next day was going to be very hot. I was dressed for yoga, my mat hanging from my shoulder. As I left my house, I looked up at the sky stretching toward the horizon. The blue was marked by a line of white tracks left by planes from the end of the world.

I was headed to the studio, excited to see Salomé, but then changed direction for no reason at all. Morris had gone abroad to work with his security friends. We had met again; he had taken me to dinner at his friend William's restaurant. I wore a little black dress and black pumps with red soles. I was nervous about making a good impression among his friends because I knew they were more like family.

Morris' friends had all come to meet me, and we stayed at the bar until closing time. Their stories made me laugh and cry, and I was immediately besotted.

That night, Morris kissed me for the first time. He dropped me off at the door, but then ran back before I went in, and he kissed me. I never wanted it to end. He carried me in his arms into the house, and gently placed me down on the bed we didn't leave for two days.

I was happy. I was so happy! This was even better than I had dreamed it could be. Does every woman wait for her Prince Charming like this? Well, I found mine.

It was time I spoke with Salomé about it.

The next day, I walked toward the yoga studio. In front of the tea room, what a shock! Sitting on the terrace, I saw Napoleon and the Empire Marshals in full costume, drinking beer.

Were they people who were not people? Wizards? I wondered. I approached them carefully. Laura, the waitress, seeing the face I was making, came towards me laughing.

"Anna, are you okay? You look like you've seen a ghost?" she asked.

"Hi, Laura! Who are these people?" I replied.

"Oh them? They're actors. There's a movie being shot in the neighborhood so they came in for a drink while on break. Would you like to sit down?" she asked.

"Oh, no, no, but thank you. I will see you later!" I said and left.

Laura waved and I smiled big in return.

Without a doubt, I was traumatized. I saw wizards everywhere! If The Healer had been there, I knew he would be laughing at me.

I noticed I felt more open. I felt like talking to people, and doing weird things like throwing myself in the snow with my arms outstretched (it was summer). I found myself believing in Santa Claus and wanting to buy fancy lingerie! My usual reserve and mistrust, instilled by my childhood, had been swept away by a tsunami.

I continued my walk, not knowing where it might lead me.

Overhead, a few birds chased each other, like two fighter planes. A third one joined them, and they guided me to the square with the beautiful fountain. Sitting on the same park bench, where he sat before with me and Salomé, I saw The Healer.

He saw me, too, and gave me a big smile, his hands in prayer. I joined my hands together, smiled back, and said "Namaste" under my breath. It means my Soul acknowledges and recognizes the Soul that is in you.

I was thinking of the Dalai Lama. *"The more meaning we give to our lives, the less regret we will feel at the moment of Death."*

His smile was radiant, and a wave of heat and tenderness overwhelmed me. I realized how much The Healer meant to me in such a short time. A few pigeons waddled at his feet like mechanical robots, probably the same ones as usually flock to him.

"Of course, Sir, I'm not going to ask if you were waiting for me, or if by chance you sent the birds to me with the Intention of guiding me here?" I joked.

"Dear Anna, reading your text about the exceptional powers of these sorcerers as described in your book, let me remind you that they are a work of fiction. And in reference to that quote earlier about the Dalai Lama: *'To*

give meaning to one's life, one needs a flawless life to have the
Energy to fight one's enemies…'"

I interrupted. "Bit sir, what enemies? I have no enemies that I know of, only friends." Even so, I got up in a hurry, feeling anxious and looking around me in case a wizard was there. The Healer started laughing.

And suddenly I realized that I had never mentioned this quote from the Dalai Lama. I had thought it in my mind, yes, but I never spoke about it to The Healer.

Holy shit! I said to myself, and noticed he was glancing at me sideways. He looked like a bird craning its neck.

My legs gave way underneath me. I slumped back down on the bench.

"Anna, don't look around for your enemies. They are inside you," he said.

"Inside me? What do you mean?" I said.

"Fear," sweet Anna. The first enemy is Fear."

"You are right, you are so right, Sir," I said. "I am afraid of everything I see these days, and all the time!"

I thought he was going to laugh at me again, but he was very serious.

"Anna! You have already done so much work on yourself. Fear disappears from your vibration when you heal" he said. "But beware. When you defeat Fear, the second enemy appears and it is just as formidable."

"Sir, you are frightening me," I said. I wanted it to come across as a joke, but I was not kidding.

The Healer did not laugh. He passed his hand over my forehead and said softly, as if he was my father. "You may have defeated Fear, my Anna, but not Clairvoyance. This is the second enemy."

His hand became heavy on my forehead, and my eyes closed. Like a spirit, I heard him tell me to rest.

"Sleep, Anna. Rest. Don't let these witch stories become an obsession."

28
ANNA, SALOMÉ AND OTHERS

"Anna! Anna, are you okay? I think you had a panic attack!" I heard Salomé say. "Wake up."

I was lying on the bench, my head on Salomé's lap.

"Salomé? Wait, I am so confused. What are you doing here? Were you here with The Healer? Did you hear me talking to him?"

My eyelids were half-open, I was in and out of consciousness.

Was I talking out loud when I said I was in love with Morris?

"Oh, Anna," she said. She had a tendril of my hair wrapped around her index finger, as she soothed me.

"I'm so sorry! Where am I? I don't know what he did to me, The Healer! He put me in a trance like this," I said.

She smiled at me like the sun, and I emerged from my mental fog. Salomé was one of those unique beings that, man or woman, one can only love her."

"It's okay, beautiful," she said. "The Healer was here with you, yes, but he had an emergency. He had someone at the far end of the world he needed to treat by Zoom, he said, so he asked me to come and sit with you until your healing was finished. The Healer said you rest, so I was happy to come and just sit with you while you rested."

"Salomé, I'm so sorry, I meant to come to yoga today, but then I saw Napoleon. And the birds brought me here to the park to find The Healer. Did I sleep for a long time?" I asked.

"What on earth are you talking about!? Napoleon?" Salomé asked.

"Good Lord! Never mind, I'll have to explain it to you later," I said.

"Well, at least you can rest assured knowing you don't snore," Salomé laughed. "Come on, now that you are awake, we must go to The Healer's house. He asked me to bring you to him as soon as you woke up."

Salomé was wearing black jeans and a white t-shirt with the word "Love" written across it. Without makeup and her long, curly brown hair tied into a ponytail, she looked like a very young girl.

"Salomé…" I said. "I need to talk to you."

"Of course," she said. "Come, let's walk and on the way to The Healer, you'll talk. Hey, why such a serious face?"

We took a shortcut, crossing under a tunnel by the expressway. The area was sketchy, so we walked rather quickly. We were almost at the end when suddenly two men appeared, blocking our exit.

"So, girls, going for a walk?" one said.

Neither of us answered, we just kept walking.

"Hey, you want some?" the man was pointing to a packet of what looked like drugs. "We'll give this to you for a very good price. We just have one favor to ask first."

As we tried to pass, the men grabbed us from behind. It all happened so fast, and before I could register what was happening, I saw Salomé kick one of the assailants in the groin. He collapsed in pain, shriveling up like a child. Then, she sent a flying elbow back into the gut of the other man. He, too, fell to the ground hunched over in pain.

That's when a third assailant attacked. It was as if he came out of the shadows. He was yielding a knife. That's when a rage I had never felt before rose up from deep inside me.

There was an iron bar lying on the ground, not too far from me. I took it and threw it with all my strength, hitting that third man from behind. "Die, scum!" I shouted.

He released his grip on Salomé and fell to the ground. She ran from behind him, strangling the man with the bar, while I kicked him with all my might between the legs.

"Come on! Let's get out of here. NOW!" Salomé yelled. I ran right behind her until we cleared the exit and made our way safely to the street. A taxi was there waiting, as if it had been sent especially for us. We jumped in and gave him The Healer's address. As I looked back, I noticed the three attackers there. Only now, it was raining and the rain turned them into wet dogs.

Catching my breath, I thought to myself that I had just defeated Clairvoyance. When I could speak again, I asked Salomé if she was alright.

"Alright? I am better than alright, are you kidding? Have you ever seen a woman so strong?" and she laughed a guttural laugh that I knew was tinged with trauma. "I bet you never thought I was capable of that," she said.

"My violent yoga teacher," I said laughing. "I am proud of you," and I took her hand in mine. As I did, I noticed her ring finger adorned with a beautiful diamond ring. I raised her hand so I could see it better.

"So, Anna, you wanted to talk to me?" she smirked.

"Salomé! You got engaged?! Oh, my goodness, congratulations!"

"I was going to tell you," she said, "but we got sidetracked. I wanted to ask if you would stand up for me at my wedding."

"I would love to!" I said.

"You don't know Claude yet, but you will love her," Salomé said. "You've seen her at yoga but I'm not sure you actually met. She is tall, brunette, has short hair and very dark skin."

"She sounds beautiful, Salomé, just like you! Tell me more about her!" I said.

"She is a brilliant doctor in nuclear physics. She teaches at the Faculty of Science," Salomé said. "Anna, you can't imagine how happy she makes me."

"Salomé, it is Claude who is the lucky one, believe me," I said. "I cannot wait for your wedding and finally to celebrate something good for a change. It will be wonderful."

The rain continued to fall but the taxi kept us safe and dry.

"Salomé… where did you learn to fight like that?" I knew the answer was Morris, but I was hoping she might say his name out loud and open the door to an easier conversation. Even after such an eventful day, I still felt nervous asking her about him.

"Morris taught me!" she said. "You can imagine, learning from someone with special forces training - there's no one better."

"Ah, Morris!" I said, feigning stupidity. "You know when I said I needed to talk to you about something? Well, I wanted to ask you about him."

"Go ahead," she said. "Ask me anything."

"I kind of like him," I said nervously. "After Morris taught class for you, I met him afterwards. We've seen each other a few times now, and, umm, but I know you two used to be together, which I didn't know when I first got together with Morris, and so…." I stumbled.

"If it makes you uncomfortable in any way, or if you object to me seeing Morris for any reason, I mean, I understand," I said. "I just need you to tell me the truth because I would never do anything to damage our friendship."

She looked at me lovingly, took my face in her hands, and kissed me on the forehead.

"You," she said. "I love you so much! And you have nothing to worry about. You have my absolute blessing."

We finally arrived in front of The Healer's house. We got out of the car and started walking up the driveway. Salomé stopped me for a moment, and took my arm.

"He didn't want me to tell you, but I'm telling you anyway," she said.

"What...?"

"Morris and I had lunch not so long ago, it was before he substituted for me in class. You know, he talked about you all the time. He wanted to know how well I knew you, and if it would be a problem if he asked you out," Salomé said.

"He did??? When?" I was dying to know.

"I told Morris how happy I would be to see him ask you out. I love him, and I love you, and I cannot imagine being happier for two people to see it work out," she said, taking me into her arms for a tight hug.

"There's only one problem," she added.

"Oh no, what..." I said, suddenly anxious.

"This is very important. Whose maid of honor would I be?" Salomé giggled like a school girl, her hand covering her mouth. I wanted to laugh with her except I was still in a state of shock.

29
DEATH, A FRIEND

"Let me summarize it for you, Anna," he said. The first enemy is Fear. When you defeat Fear, the second enemy appears, Clairvoyance. After Clairvoyance comes Power."

We were seated in the living room. The Healer was helping me recover from the shock of meeting those thugs.

"How did it feel, Anna? Meeting multiple enemies at once?" The Healer asked me.

"You mean in the fight with those thugs?" I asked.

"Well, yes. Power gives us a sense of invincibility and security that can be illusory and dangerous. In fact, it is said that the Wise Men, with advanced degrees of absolute power, are the ones who most easily lose it," The Healer said.

He continued. "When you defeat Power, Wisdom comes. Peace follows, and then finally, Old Age. One can delay the Old Age, naturally, but it can never be truly defeated. Only Death can do that.

"Isn't Death an enemy?" I asked.

He looked at me for a long time, and said softly.

Death, my dear Anna is our best friend. Death is our guide. She shows us how to love Life more than anything else because once Life is gone, there is nothing left. When Death takes you, everything in this Life ends. The solace comes in knowing there are many other future lives waiting for us," The Healer said in a contemplative voice.

"The Soul has a long journey," he said.

"I know this for a fact. I have practiced Past Life Regression many times myself and I have done it for many of my clients," The Healer said with certainty. "Death is the pathway to another Life... and the only pathway there is Love. Love is the way!"

"Some say that for those whose Lives have been flawless, Death lets them do their last dance in their favorite place. Death waits until they are finished to seize them," he said.

I noticed a tear fall from The Healer's eye. His eyes were bright and his face lit up by the sun coming in from the window. He raised his hand to protect his eyes from the light.

"That's how it must have been for my parents," he said lovingly. "And I hope it will be the same for me when my time comes."

Lowering his hand, he offered his face to the sun and took a deep breath. It was like watching him inhale and swallow the light. I felt the urge to do the same, and as I took in a deep, cleansing breath, I felt intense emotions wash over me: Sadness, Clarity, Healing and Love.

"Sit closer to me," he said, rolling the white chair over to me. "We will do your last healing in this magical sunset. Remember, dusk and dawn are breaches between worlds," he said.

And the ballet of his hands began. He controlled my chakras with his pendulum. The wooden ball turned at the end of a black thread. He held the pendulum with his right hand as his left hand waved back and forth over my body. With each wave, I felt an intense vibration.

The setting sun illuminated the scene. The living room became a surreal orange color. Our shadows lengthened on the floor and walls. I understood the breach was closing, we were leaving day and entering night.

We took three small breaks. I drank a glass of water next to me, listening to the sound of the World breathing.

In the last clearing, his hands made big circles around me. He did not touch me. I felt his vibrations drawing out my Aura even so.

"Anna! Your Aura has taken on its full amplitude and true colors!" he said.

He outstretched his arms, with his palms face down in front of me. He told me to place my palms over his without touching him. The heat rose so quickly throughout my body. I noticed as the Energy moved up and down, from my shoulders to my solar plexus, it lingered there.

He removed his hands. I remained seated, as if in another world. I had never felt his Energy that intensely before. As it retreats, a certain calm wash over me. I am no longer able to think. Instead, I feel.

30
CLAUDE

WHAT ABOUT CRISTALS

Slowly, I regained consciousness and opened my eyes. It was dark outside and I found myself alone in the living room. Slowly and deliberately, I got up from my chair and headed down the hall. I heard noise coming from another room and decided to follow it.

There, I found The Healer sitting on a sofa. He was talking to Morris, who had a drink in his hand. Salomé and Claude sat on the sofa across from them. They didn't see me standing there in the shadows. I listened to their conversation.

"Do I believe in God?" asked The Healer. "But of course! The imprint of the Divine is everywhere. I see it in every gesture of my hands."

"How so?" Claude asked.

The Healer stood up. "With Love, of course! How else? Love is the way to Energy, it is Energy itself! Claude, you know this from teaching that Energy is God, Love and Quantum Physics!"

Claude was stunning. She was of Masai background. Her dark skin radiated in the bright green dress she wore, showing off her long legs.

She stood up, like The Healer, and took over becoming the professor she was. The living room transformed into an amphitheater, and with great presence, took center stage.

"Sir, quantum physics has made it possible to highlight what is known as the zero-point field or vacuum Energy," she said. "In the blink of an eye, an exchange of Energy between subatomic particles creates more virtual particles. Though the exchange itself represents the smallest amount of energy, when we add up the subatomic particles across all elements of the Universe, we arrive at an unimaginable amount of Energy."

She continued. "We are all connected to this giant Energy field, even at the farthest reaches of the universe. This is how healers work. They can connect to this vacuum Energy and transmit a healing by Intention."

I walked into the room and sat down next to Morris.

"But Claude, what is the link with Love, the Spiritual, the Religious, and God?" Morris asked her.

"It is a good question," she said. "We interpret relative quantum theory as a vacuum of virtual particles passing through a potential state of Energy. They are not considered subatomic particles since one cannot observe them, but does that make it so?" Claude said.

I wondered if the rest of the room understood what I did not.

"Lao-tzu, the founder of Taoism, defines emptiness as being full of potential. The Spiritual is this way, it is about being fully present. I imagine it as a connection between the Taoist vacuum and the potential of relative quantum physics," Claude said.

"I am with you, Claude," The Healer said. "Do you know Father Pierre Teilhard de Chardin?" he asked, and without waiting for a reply, began quoting him from memory.

> *"It is no longer a question of the application of human faculties to this or that deity... We are beginning to understand that the only religion acceptable to man is the one that will first teach him to recognize, love, and passionately serve the universe, of which he is the most important element."*

"It always comes back to Love, doesn't it?" I said, quoting the Prophet of Khalil Gibran:

> *Love gives only of itself and takes only of itself.*

Love does not possess, and does not want to be possessed.

For love is enough for love.'"

Everyone looked at me, smiling. Their faces were luminous. In Morris' arms,

I nearly burst into tears, overwhelmed by the happiness I felt in that moment.

"Sir, I nearly forgot!" Salome said. "Remember Claire, and how you told us to remind you to tell us her story?"

- Oh yes, of course Anna! Thank you for reminding me, this story is a good example of people who are not so intriguing

Claire's restaurant was on the shore of a lake at the entrance of a town famous for its mineral water.

It was during a visit to a friend that I met her.

The tables in front of the bay were illuminated by the setting sun and on this summer Saturday evening they should have been full of customers, but unfortunately this was far from being the case.

Knowing my friend Paula well, I quickly realized that I had not come just to dine and enjoy the view. At the end of the dinner Claire came to sit with us.

- It was excellent Madam... I feel your distress, as they say: "The Friends of my Friends are my Friends" I am at your disposal to help you!...

-Thank you, Sir, but please call me Claire, I had asked Paula not to tell you anything to leave your perception free, as you see the restaurant is almost empty and the staff does not stay ...

The chefs come and go and often I end up alone in the kitchen, which causes major delays in service, and even if the place is very beautiful! The customers don't come back.

I'm cursed, not to mention tired, I'm raising my little girl alone, I don't understand what's going on.

- Have you been in business for long?

- No, just a year! Before, I had a bistro that was doing well, but I was seduced by the beauty of the place and its location, which allowed me to double my income and live there, so I sold the bistro and bought this business.

- Claire is a young woman usually full of energy and energy says Paula to me but there it is as if she was turned off, I do not recognize her...

- Cursed, I tell you, I am from the South, I know it Sir, it seems that the person who was here before me practiced a form of black magic, he was fired by the condominium, in fact he wanted to stay and was angry to be forced to leave! Come sir, I will show you around and you will see for yourself what you perceive!

-My dear friends, the visit was conclusive, the interior of the restaurant, from the kitchen to the reception, was inhabited by negative entities called by the former operator, these people who were not people, right Anna?

- I interrupted him... But Sir, what did you do?

- I placed Clear Quartz crystals in every place where they were needed Anna, and gave a crystal necklace to Claire and Paula with instructions to say prayers,

Each of these prayers must be accompanied by a very strong vibration of Love for these creatures who are often in darkness.

We started on the first night and I can tell you that the vibration had purified considerably.

The Healer stood up and came to lean against the table next to Claude.

- What do you know about crystals? he said.

- Look! We are wearing all the crystals you gave us, clear Quartz! Said Myriam

Indeed, I was wearing mine around my neck, long and set-in silver irons similar to that of Morris and the Healer, Myriam and Claude each had transparent crystals set in gold wire worn in the form of a ring.

To my great surprise Morris got up and went to join the Healer and Claude came to sit next to Myriam, the beauty of their silhouette and the graphism of their long legs in the contrast of the color of their skin was magnificent reminding me of a surrealist photo of Guy Bourdin.

There is so much beauty in this world for those who know how to look and I was looking at Morris, he was beautiful, taking his time to unfold a printed sheet of paper that he had taken out of the inside pocket of his jacket.

- My friends!" said Morris. The Healer has asked me to present you with some information about the Crystal we carry...

 The Clear Quartz.

Morris smiled at me and cleared his throat and start to reed :

Clear Quartz works on three levels.

- Energy amplification,

- Ability to receive programming

- Ability to be remembered

It can be programmed through focused intention to help us achieve our goals in our inner and outer lives.

The key words are:

Programmable, amplification of intentions, expansion of ambient energies, clearing, cleansing, healing, memory and Chakra enhancement.

With a Clear Quartz during Meditation, we can visualize an image of our intention or desired outcome within the Crystal and this will have a powerful psychic amplification effect.

After such a session, especially if we practice the same programming over and over again,

with the same crystal, many inner and outer events will seem to occur in sync to achieve the manifestation of our desire.

The fact that the Crystal program "remembers" the power of our desire and amplifies it can greatly assist us in "holding the pattern" of energy long enough and with enough force for manifestation to occur.

Clear Quartz is a Stone of Light, giving the one who meditates with it, greater spiritual clarity. It provides a clear corridor for vibrational frequencies.

Sleeping with Clear Quartz can increase the clarity of dreams and holding a Clear Quartz will often intensify the experience of Meditation.

Clear Quartz can be used to amplify the energies of other stones, to make tools and energy grids.

It is a tool for healing, expanding consciousness, opening chakras, balancing polarities, communicating with guides, remembering past lives, and just about anything else you can imagine.

We are unlimited beings, in our minds.

We can even program it to enhance our imagination!

It also serves to clear and cleanse our own energies!

Clear Quartz is a cardinal ally of the element of Storm, functioning at all levels of the energetic and physical bodies, and resonating with all chakras.

As such, it is most active on the nervous system and connective tissues of the body. Its structure and frequency range allow it to amplify any energy with which it resonates. It is therefore an excellent ally for healing and prayer work.

Clear Quartz embodies the concepts of clarity and the utility of becoming a vessel for the Light of the Divine.

It thus introduces clear thought and purpose into our minds and hearts, and can help us overcome confusion.

It helps establish a strong link with higher guidance, amplifying communication on the higher planes.

It can then be used to enhance telepathic communication and stimulate paranormal vision.

Clear Quartz crystals are storage devices that can be "programmed" or made to resonate with any thoughts or emotions we wish to broadcast more strongly into the world. Once a crystal has been programmed in this way, it will continue to resonate with that thought, prayer or emotion, continually broadcasting that energy through the Earth's electromagnetic field and into the etheric realms.

On the Spiritual Level:

Clear Quartz encourages clarity on all planes. We can use it to enhance communication with guides and amplify paranormal abilities. It works to stimulate and open the chakras as well as the circulation pathways in the body, giving rise to a larger, more enlightened auric field.

Emotionally:

Clear Quartz is emotionally neutral but will amplify any emotion it resonates with.

Physical Level:

Clear Quartz stimulates the nervous system as well as nail and hair growth. It can help eliminate adhesions in connective tissue.

Morris puts his paper back in his inside jacket pocket and says :

- That, dear Friends, was a summary of what I was able to gather on the Clear Quartz Crystal, by searching various sources, of course proofread and verified by the Healer.

We applaud him warmly and this man, this brave and fearless fighter, starts to blush like a shy girl, moved, I stand up and extend my arms to him. After greeting us with folded hands, he came and sat down next to me.

On the table, there were small blue books where it was written

"Psalms of David".

And a bottle with a crystal inside filled with champagne, suchis and glasses were waiting for us...

The Healer took one of the little blue books in his hand and said...

- Friends! Prayer is THE VIBRATION!

I particularly recommend the Psalm of David, number 23, with infinitely powerful Kabbalistic energy, which you will find in the books in front of you,

I suggest you recite it together, to bring to our evening a spiritual food at the height of the very material one which awaits us.

— *The LORD is my shepherd; I shall not want. He makes me to lie down in green pastures; He leads me beside the still waters. He restores my soul; He leads me in the paths of righteousness For His name's sake. Yea, though I walk through the valley of the shadow of death, I will fear no evil; For You are with me; Your rod and Your staff, they comfort me. You prepare a table before me in the presence of my enemies; You anoint my head with oil; My cup runs over. Surely goodness and mercy shall follow me All the days of my life; And I will dwell in the house of the LORD Forever —*

We stood up, pressed together.

The Healer, with folded hands, looked at us for a long time...

His eyes shone with Love.

By magic coming from elsewhere, we could hear

Leonard Cohen singing ...

"Alleluia".

***

TABLE OF CONTENTS

Made in United States
Orlando, FL
12 October 2022